# Dawn's Book

**Other books by**
**Ann M. Martin**

*Rachel Parker, Kindergarten Show-off*
*Eleven Kids, One Summer*
*Ma and Pa Dracula*
*Yours Turly, Shirley*
*Ten Kids, No Pets*
*Slam Book*
*Just a Summer Romance*
*Missing Since Monday*
*With You and Without You*
*Me and Katie (the Pest)*
*Stage Fright*
*Inside Out*
*Bummer Summer*

BABY-SITTERS LITTLE SISTER series
THE BABY-SITTERS CLUB mysteries
THE BABY-SITTERS CLUB series

# *Dawn's Book*

Ann M. Martin

SCHOLASTIC INC.
New York Toronto London Auckland Sydney

*The author gratefully acknowledges*
*Jeanne Betancourt*
*for her help in*
*preparing this manuscript.*

Interior art and cover drawing by Angelo Tillery

Cover painting by Hodges Soileau



ISBN 0-590-22864-1



12 11 10 9 8 7 6 5 4 3 2 5 6 7 8 9/9 0/0

Printed in the U.S.A. 40

First Scholastic printing, September 1995

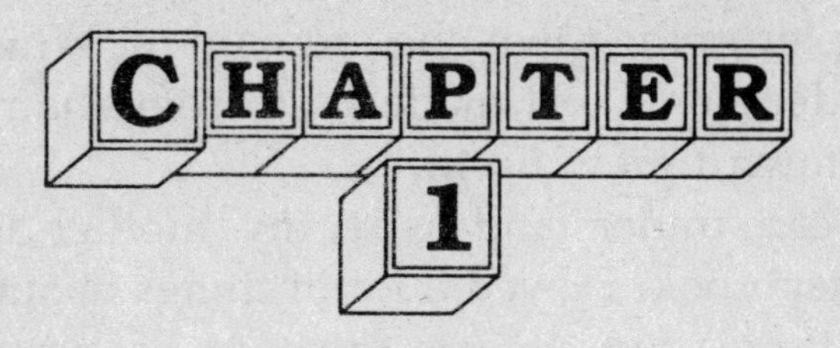

I woke up wondering, Where am I? I opened my eyes and looked around my sunny California bedroom and remembered that I'm back on the West Coast. And this time it's for good.

Not long ago I moved here from Connecticut (on the East Coast) where I lived with my mother; her second husband, Richard; and his daughter, Mary Anne. (Mary Anne also happens to be one of my best friends.) Now I'm going to live with my father; his new wife, Carol; and my ten-year-old brother, Jeff. Pretty confusing, huh?

"Dawn, honey, time to get up." The cheerful voice coming from the hallway was my dad's. He's really happy that I decided to move back home with him and Jeff. I was born in California and lived here (mostly in this house) until my parents split up. That's when my mother, Jeff, and I moved to Stoneybrook, Connecticut. My mother grew up in Stoneybrook and her parents still live there. With all the divorce troubles my mother felt she'd be happier in the town she grew up in. Which is the decision I just made — to come home to the town I grew up in.

I can understand why my mother loves Stoneybrook. I loved a lot of things about living there, too. It was great to be near my grandparents, Granny and Pop-Pop. And I made friends with a fabulous group of girls right away. They even invited me to join their baby-sitting club. The members of the Baby-sitters Club are definitely the best friends a person could want. And the kids we baby-sat for were terrific, too.

"Knock, knock." That was Jeff knocking on my bedroom door and calling out the first line of one of his dumb jokes. Instead of saying, "Who's there?" I replied, "Knock, knock."

Jeff was on the ball this morning and called back, "Banana," skipping the "Who's there?" part entirely.

I completed the joke. "Orange you glad I didn't say banana?" I said, opening the door.

Frankenstein was standing in front of me! I screamed before I realized that it was only Jeff in a rubber Halloween mask.

Jeff was thrilled.

Jeff is also happy that we're living together

full-time now. He missed me a lot. Especially when my dad became serious about one of the women he was dating and decided to marry her. My new stepmother is younger than my dad. I had trouble with Carol at first, but I like her a lot better now that she's not trying so hard to make me like her.

I dressed and went to the kitchen for breakfast. Carol was already dressed for work and eating granola and yogurt. We said good morning to one another, but Carol seemed distracted. As I fed oranges into the juicer she asked, "Have you seen my Rollerblades, Dawn?" (I told you she was younger than my dad.)

"Uh-uh," I answered. "Where did you take them off last?"

"Maybe it was in the car," she said. "Or was it at work?"

Hearing Carol talk like this made me miss my mother. Mom is the queen of absent-mindedness and is probably the least-organized person I know. Fortunately her second husband, my friend Mary Anne Spier's father, is extremely organized. He and Mom seem to balance one another without driving each other crazy.

Don't get the idea that because I don't live with my mother I don't get along with her.

My mom's great. We're going to miss one another tons. It was hard to leave her and my friends in Stoneybrook. But now that I'm back in California I know I made the right decision. Someplace deep inside me I feel happy. When I was in Stoneybrook I kept getting the nagging feeling that I wasn't in the right place. The right place for me is California.

My dad walked into the kitchen. "You making some orange juice, Sunshine?" he asked me. I put a glass of fresh juice at his place and he put a manila folder at mine.

"What's that?" I asked.

"A few things that I saved over the years," he said. "I thought you might be able to use them."

The tab on the folder read *Sunshine.* You've probably figured out that Sunshine is my dad's nickname for me. I opened the folder. It was chock-full of announcements, newspaper clippings, old report cards, and class photos.

I jumped up and gave my dad a kiss. "Thanks. This is exactly what I needed for my autobiography."

Yes, I've been writing my autobiography. It was the first homework assignment I got on my first day back at my old school, Vista. I have to write the story of my life so far. All my old friends in Stoneybrook have been given the same assignment. Here's what's really funny. At my going-away party they teased me about moving to California just so I wouldn't have to do that assignment. I'm beginning to think there is a national law that says "All eighth-grade students shall write their autobiographies."

I finished breakfast and told Carol that if she couldn't find her Rollerblades she could borrow mine. Then I kissed my dad good-bye and headed over to Sunny Winslow's house. Sunny, my best California friend, lives only two doors away from us. I always stop by her place on the way to school and we walk together. I've gone through the Winslows' kitchen door thousands of times in my life.

Today Mrs. Winslow was sitting at the kitchen table drinking tea. Mrs. Winslow is one of my favorite people in the whole world. And she has cancer. No one can say for sure if she'll get better. She had an operation and now she has chemotherapy appointments at the hospital every week. One of the reasons I wanted to move back to California was to be near Sunny and her parents.

I knocked lightly on the screen door and walked inside. Mrs. Winslow looked up and smiled. "It's so wonderful to have you back here," she said in a weak but cheery voice. It's only eight o'clock in the morning and for about the twentieth time since I woke up I'm reminded that moving back to California was the right decision.

Sunny came bouncing into the room. "Dawn," she said, "I can't believe we're walking to school together again."

"Me, too," I said.

"Me, three," said Mrs. Winslow with a wink.

The school day went great. I love Vista. Except for the time I lived in Stoneybrook, I've been at Vista since first grade. I have lots of good friends here, but my best friends are Sunny, Jill Henderson, and Maggie Blume.

Maggie Blume has a very cool look. She wears her hair spikey in front. In the back she has a long thin tail which she streaks in black or a bright color like green or purple. Maggie doesn't act like a rich kid, but she is one. You'd know it if you saw her house. It has dozens of rooms, including a gym and a screening room. Maggie's dad is in the movie business and famous people hang out at her place all the time. But Maggie doesn't care about that and hangs out with us "ordinary" folks.

Jill Henderson has dark blonde hair and eyes that are deep chocolate brown. Her parents are divorced and she lives with her mom and her older sister. My friends and I love to surf, but Jill's really good at it. She's the most serious of my California friends, and the quietest. In that way she reminds me of my stepsister Mary Anne.

Sunny Winslow is my very best California friend. Her personality is just like her name — sunny. She's outgoing, independent, and fun-loving. But I know she can't be too happy when her mother is so sick.

Here's a bit about me. I have long blonde hair and am physically fit. I love to surf and eat healthy foods. I'm one of those people who thinks that tofu and raw veggies are treats and hates sweets and fatty foods. I have a laid back attitude toward life, which means I take things as they come.

After school Maggie, Jill, Sunny, and I walked out of the building together. We were going to Sunny's house for our weekly We ♥ Kids Club meeting.

I better explain. I already mentioned that in Stoneybrook I was a member (and an officer) of the Baby-sitters Club. Well, Sunny started a baby-sitting club in California. It's called We ♥ Kids. The club in Stoneybrook is extremely well-organized. The members hold three regular meetings a week, and have lots of rules, officers, and a notebook that everyone has to write in and read every week. The BSC works really well. So does W♥KC. But there're a lot of differences in the way the two clubs are run. W♥KC is not very organized. We don't have officers and rules. We don't even mind if someone is a little late for a meeting. (The BSC founder and president, Kristy Thomas, has a *fit* if anyone is late for a meeting.)

"Is it all right that we're meeting at your house with your mom sick and everything?" I asked Sunny. "Maybe we should meet at my house."

"Mom said she likes having us around," Sunny said.

"Let's stop and get her some flowers," I suggested.

Mrs. Winslow loved the pink roses that we brought her. "Why, thank you," she said with a big smile. I could see that Sunny was right about her mother liking that we were there. Even though Mrs. Winslow felt sick, she prepared us a great snack — a big platter of snow peas and cherry tomatoes from her garden with a dip made of homemade yogurt and fresh herbs. "This is the first time I've gone out to the garden since I got home from the hospital," she told us. "Being there reminded me that my garden is a healing place."

I gave her a hug. "I'm so glad you've come home," she whispered to me.

"Me, too," I whispered back.

We held the meeting in the living room so we could spread out. The first call was from Mrs. Austin, asking me to sit for her daughters, Clover and Daffodil, on Saturday night. My very first sitting job ever was for Clover and Daffodil. I love these kids, so I said I would take the job. Sunny entered that in our record book while I braided Maggie's green tail. When the phone rang a second time, Jill answered. "Hi," she said. (If this were a BSC meeting in Stoneybrook she'd answer, "Hello, Baby-sitters Club.")

Jill asked us if anyone was free to sit for the Waldens on Friday after school. "I can," Maggie said.

Sunny checked the book and confirmed that Maggie was free. Jill told Mrs. Walden that Maggie would be there. It was as simple as that.

We got a couple more calls during the meeting, but basically we had a gab session and ate veggies and dip.

After the meeting I went home and worked on my autobiography. I reread what I'd done so far and began to fit in the things Dad had given me that morning.

I worked on the project until dinnertime. After dinner I worked on it some more. I didn't mind. I thought my life so far was pretty interesting.

# The Life and Times of Dawn Read Schafer: Bicoastal Girl

## West Coast Beginnings

I was born at St. Mary's Hospital in Anaheim, California. I was due to be born on January 28th. But I skipped being born that day. I skipped it the next day, too. And the day after that.

A week later my mother was still pregnant. That's when she got this idea that if she went for a long walk on the beach it just might help move things along.

There is a brand new day dawning for
Sharon and Jack Schafer.
Dawn Read Schafer
born February 5th at 6:45 a.m.


*My mom and dad tell the world that I am here.*

The beach was crowded with swimmers and surfers that day. My mother says she felt pretty silly walking around with a belly as big as a beachball. But she was convinced that the sound of the sea and the pull of the tides would do the trick.

For hours she and my dad walked and rested on the beach. About the time the sun went down and the tide went out, she told my dad it was time to go to the hospital. And that's where I was born at dawn the next morning.

My mother thinks that my love for the sea started because she spent the afternoon and evening before I was born at the beach. She might be right. Anyway, to this day I am drawn to the ocean. I love everything about it. Put me on a sandy beach where I can hear the pounding surf, smell the salt water, and look out at blue water meeting blue sky, and I am in heaven.

My parents took me to the beach a lot during the first year of my life. They'd put me on a blanket under the beach umbrella. If I got fussy all they had to do was dip me in the ocean. In an instant my mood would change from mad or sad to glad.

Here's the story my dad tells about when I took my first step.

By the time I was a year old I'd figured out how to stand and walk while holding onto things. So Dad decided it was time for me to walk on my own. One day when he returned from work he stood me at the coffee table. Then he backed away from me, squatted, and held out his arms. "Come on, Sunshine," he cooed. "Come to Daddy."

I smiled, gave him a little goo-goo ga-ga, but didn't let go of the table. Every night that week my father would stand me at the coffee

*One ... two... three ... A dip in the sea.*

table and encourage me to walk to him. Every night I'd make my safe way around the table.

That Sunday we went to the beach. While my parents were lounging on our beach blanket reading the Sunday papers, I pulled myself upright by holding onto our picnic cooler. My parents complimented me on my feat and returned to their papers. A minute later my dad looked up to check on me, but I wasn't there. After briefly thinking I'd been stolen, he saw me taking wobbly steps on the beach. He got my mother's attention and they quietly walked behind me to see how far I would go on my first upright journey.

I took a few more steps to where the sand met the sea and plopped myself down. My parents say I splashed the water with my hands and laughed.

According to my baby book my first words were:

Wa-wa (water)
Ma-ma (mother)
Da-da (father)
Be-ee (beach)

Don't think I was some bizarre kid you could make a weird movie about called *Baby from the Sea* or something. I loved all sorts of regular toddler stuff. The playground, for example. I liked to go back and forth on the swings or swish down the slide. But my favorite playground activity was seesawing with my mother and me on one end, and my dad balancing us on the other end. Now that I think about it, the feeling you get on a seesaw is a little like riding waves. And Mom says that whenever I got near the sandbox I'd cry for the "be-ee" and the "wa-wa." Am I sounding weird again?

Well, I wasn't. I was a normal kid with a roomful of normal kid toys. I especially liked to build things with Legos and to make things out of Play-Doh. I thought Play-Doh was the neatest stuff. I'd wander around the house putting it in all sorts of places, which meant my mother would find it in all sorts of places.

One day she went to the fridge to get out a dish of vegetarian chili we were going to have for dinner. A big clump of white stuff was floating in it. By the time she'd put the dish on the table she'd guessed that the white stuff was Play-Doh. She led me from the living room where I was building a Lego lifeguard stand to the table. She fished out the Play-Doh with a wooden spoon and put it on a paper towel. "Dawn, what's this?" she asked sternly.

"Sou cre," I answered (translation: sour cream). Before she knew what was happening

I picked up the messy clump and put it back where it belonged — in the chili. I smiled, repeated "sou cre," and returned to my construction project in the living room. My mother says she couldn't scold me because if she'd opened her mouth she would have started laughing.

Raising me gave my mom some scary moments, too. One afternoon I was playing alone in my room. When Mom came in with some clean laundry she saw bright red coming out of my ears. "Dawn," she said in as calm a tone as she could manage, "let Mommy look in your ears."

"Huh?" I asked. Mom forgot calm and ran to me. Her precious girl couldn't hear! Fortunately she took a closer look before she dialed 911. My ears were stuffed with red Play-Doh. I tried to pull her hand away from my ear. "MY ear-tings," I cried. *"Mine."*

As she pulled out the Play-Doh, she realized that "ear-tings" were "earrings." And that when I couldn't get my "earrings" to stay on my earlobes, I'd pushed them into my ears.

She took me to the pediatrician to be sure that all the Play-Doh was out. The doctor thought it was pretty funny. My mother did not. To this day she can't stand the sight or smell of Play-Doh. But I still love it and use it a lot when I baby-sit for young kids.

When I was three years old I got the biggest surprise of my life. It started when my parents weren't there to put me to bed at night. They still weren't there when I woke up in the morning. That day Granny and Pop-Pop flew all the way across the country to stay with us. Still no Mommy or Daddy. When my parents finally came home they were not alone. Mom was carrying a bundle that moved and cried and that everyone called "the baby." I was confused. I thought I was the baby! Well, it didn't take me long to figure out that I wasn't the center of everyone's attention anymore. My whole world had changed. Even my dad's pet name for me changed. Instead of calling me "Sunshine," he called me "Dawn don't."

"Dawn don't get too close to the baby."

"Dawn don't put Play-Doh on the baby's face."

"Dawn don't throw toys in the baby's crib."

"Dawn don't feed the baby your ice cream."

For awhile there didn't seem to be any sunshine in my life. My sun had set. And a new sun had risen for my parents — a *son.*

My parents insist that they didn't ignore me when Jeff was a baby. They say they were just so busy with a newborn that they couldn't give me the kind of attention I'd come to expect. Now that I've baby-sat for families in which one of the children is an infant, I know they're

*Guess who feels left out?*

right. I also realize that my brother is a kid who knows how to get attention. He probably developed that talent at an early age.

Things picked up considerably for me when I started nursery school. I loved the different activities there. My favorites were the make-believe trunk and the blocks corner. (My *least* favorite place in the nursery school was the baby doll corner.) For awhile my first choice activity was building with blocks. The block corner was well-stocked with wooden blocks in different sizes, colors, and shapes.

My partner in block building was Ruthie Robillard. Now that I'm remembering Ruthie, I realize that she was like Mary Anne, very organized and quiet. I had a lot of fun with Ruthie. Especially in that building-block corner.

Ruthie and I were big fans of the Madeline books by Ludwig Bemelmans. In case you don't know the books, Madeline is a little orphan girl from Paris who marches with her fellow orphans in two straight lines behind their teacher, Miss Clavel. They travel all over Paris this way. Madeline has many adventures.

Inspired by Madeline's adventures, Ruthie and I built our version of the city of Paris out of blocks and acted out her stories with twelve clothespin dolls. One day we were still building the Eiffel Tower when our teacher, Mrs. Anderson, clapped her hands three times. "Time to switch places, children," she instructed. "Everyone gets a turn."

I saw Harry Sterns and Jackie Rubens eyeing our Eiffel Tower.

"But we're not finished," I told Mrs. Anderson.

"Dawn, you and Ruthie join Lydia and Nicole for some dress-up," Mrs. Anderson said. "It's time for Harry and Jackie to have a turn at blocks."

My heart sank. As Ruthie and I walked away from our Paris we knew what would happen next. And it did. *Crash*. Harry and Jackie had demolished our beautiful Eiffel Tower.

Three days in a row we built our tower. Three days in a row it was demolished by the Destructive Duo.

On the third day, as Paris lay in ruins in the block corner, Ruthie and I were trying to make ourselves feel better at the make-believe trunk. She was transforming herself into a pink princess and I was wearing an old Wonder Woman Halloween costume. As I put on my Wonder Woman power bracelets, I told Ruthie, "We need a secret weapon." A few minutes later I came up with one. When I explained my idea to the Pink Princess she hesitated for a moment. Then she agreed and we made a plan.

The next day our work on the Eiffel Tower went slower than ever.

When Mrs. Anderson came by to check on us, I held the secret weapon behind my back and smiled at her.

"Well, well," she said. "You two certainly do like the Eiffel Tower. Has either of you been to Paris?"

We shook our heads no.

"Mrs. Anderson," I said in my sweetest voice, "could we have story-in-a-circle next?"

"Please," Ruthie begged. "And read Madeline. She lived in Paris. She loved the Eiffel Tower, just like us."

"You read stories so beautiful," I added.

"Well, my goodness," Mrs. Anderson said, "aren't you two sweet! I guess we could move storytime up just for today. That way you can show the other children your Eiffel Tower."

When Mrs. Anderson left us to break up a fight in the puppet center, Ruthie and I exchanged a smile and went back to work building the tower with our secret weapon — glue. By the time Mrs. Anderson clapped her hands three times and announced story-in-a-circle, we'd finished.

I couldn't believe our luck. Storytime meant

the glue had time to dry before the Destructive Duo's lethal kicks.

When storytime was over, Mrs. Anderson said, "What a shame that Dawn's and Ruthie's beautiful tower has to come down. But that's the way blocks work, isn't it, children?" She smiled at Ruthie and me. "Would you two like to take it down yourselves?"

Ruthie and I shook our heads no.

"All right then," Mrs. Anderson said. "Ruthie and Dawn go to the kitchen corner. Who wants to play with the blocks next?"

Jackie and Harry yelled, "Me, me." In an instant they'd charged over to the block corner, pulled back their right legs, and kicked hard.

"Ow!" Harry yelled.

"Hey!" Jackie exclaimed.

They kicked again. This time the tower fell — in one piece. Everyone, including Mrs. Anderson, looked at Ruthie and me.

Ruthie and I spent the rest of the morning soaking the blocks in water and wiping off the glue. A whole hour playing in water! It didn't feel like a punishment to me.

Still, Ruthie and I avoided the block corner for the rest of the year.

Each day when I came home from nursery school, my baby brother would smile and coo for me. I was the first person he ever smiled for. And the first person he walked to without holding on to anything. Jeff's first word was Da-da. I know Da-da usually means "Daddy," but for Jeff it meant "Dawn."

I learned to like having a little brother. It was fun to live with someone who adored me and followed me around. And at that early age Jeff got it into his head that it was his job to entertain me. He'd make silly faces and coo for me. I'd laugh and he'd be happy. He still thinks that he's supposed to entertain me (and anyone else he's around). Only now he does it with jokes — usually bad ones. If Jeff Schafer becomes a professional comedian, it'll be because of me.

All in all I think I'm lucky to have a brother. It taught me at an early age that the sun does not rise and set on me alone, even though my name *is* Dawn. But I like my name, and I love when my dad calls me Sunshine or hums the song, "You Are the Sunshine of My Life."

I learned another thing about myself during my early years. I adore the ocean. When I'm old enough to live on my own I will most definitely live by the sea.

# The New Girl on the Block

When I was six years old we moved to a new house in Palo City. I was heartbroken to leave Ruthie and my old neighborhood. My parents said that there would be lots of kids for me to play with in our new neighborhood. What they didn't say was that all those kids were three years old or younger.

My brother Jeff loved our new neighborhood. There were plenty of kids his age, which at that time was three. I was six and didn't have a lot in common with three-year-olds. To tell the truth, they weren't that interested in playing with me either.

Don't get me wrong. I wasn't an antisocial kid. I made plenty of friends at Vista, my new school. My friends in first grade (they're still my friends today) were Jill Henderson and Maggie Blume. Our teacher, Mr. Richards, was very laid back and let kids sit wherever they wanted. So Jill, Maggie, and I always sat together. As soon as we learned how to write, we wrote notes to one another. Which is pretty funny because in Mr. Richards' class you could talk to your friends almost anytime you wanted, so you didn't have to write notes.

A lot of our secret notes were about my yellow parakeet, Buzz. Buzz was an amazing bird. We let him fly freely around the house. There were two reasons we could do this. One was that Buzz always went back to his cage to do his bathroom business. The second was he would never fly away. He stayed in the house. And if I were there he stayed near me. Maggie and Jill were so fascinated by Buzz that I started exaggerating his feats and even made some up.

I loved playing with Jill and Maggie (I still do). But there was a problem. Neither of them lived near me. I longed for a best friend who lived on my block. I wanted to be able to run over to my friend's house early on a Saturday morning and say, "What'll we do today?"

A year went by and there still weren't any kids my age on my block. Then I noticed a FOR SALE sign on a lawn just a few houses down the street from us. The Holders and their one-year-old twins had moved! Maybe, I thought hopefully, a girl my age will move into that house. Every day after school I'd walk up and down the block a few times to see if someone was looking at that house. If they had a girl my age I was going to tell them it was a nice, quiet street and that they were looking at the prettiest house on the block.

One day I saw a man slap a SOLD sticker on the FOR SALE sign. I ran to him and asked if he'd bought the house and whether he had any kids. "I'm the real estate agent," he said. "A couple from Oregon bought this place. But I do believe they have a little girl who's just about your age."

I skipped all the way home. I couldn't believe my good luck. I was going to have a friend my own age on my very own block.

Summer vacation had started so I didn't have much to do that week but wait for her to move in. I located Oregon on my puzzle map of the United States and imagined my new friend traveling all the way down the coast from Oregon to Palo City. At least four times a day I dodged Big Wheels and strollers to walk by the empty house.

On Saturday I finally saw what I'd been waiting for. A moving van was parked in the driveway. I walked toward it trying to look nonchalant. The next thing I noticed was a strange-looking car driving down our block. When I say "strange" I don't mean strange as in "unfamiliar." I mean "strange" as in *"weird."* The car was a small, banged-up red thing painted all over with brightly colored flowers and white peace symbols. A plastic flower bobbed on the tip of the radio antenna. This bizarre-looking car pulled up in front of the house.

I knelt on one knee and pretended my shoelace was untied so it wouldn't look as if I were watching to see who would get out of the car. A man with a ponytail and a long-haired woman in an ankle-length dress stepped out of the front. "Here we are at last," the man said to the woman. "Our new home of peace and love." Peace and love? Were they turning the house into a church?

The girl I'd been waiting for — longing for — finally climbed out of the backseat. She had long blonde hair and wore an ankle-length dress, too. At that time I didn't know any kids or adults who wore long skirts, unless they wore fancy gowns in a wedding. To me that girl and her mother looked as if they were wearing nightgowns. Especially since they were barefoot.

The woman ran onto the front lawn, flung out her arms and danced in circles. The girl did the same. And then, to my horror, so did the man. As they danced on the lawn I untied my other shoelace and watched.

When the new people stopped dancing they

hugged one another. Then the man headed toward the moving van. I don't think he noticed — or cared — that the moving men were laughing at them. These were definitely the weirdest people I had ever seen outside of characters on television programs. The woman returned to the car. She called out, "Sunshine, help me with the plants."

I was stunned. This stranger knew my special nickname that only my dad used. *And* she expected me to help her. I had a spooky feeling as I walked up the driveway toward her. The girl was walking toward the woman, too.

The woman handed the girl a funny-looking plant in an old teapot. "Isn't this a pretty street, Sunshine?" she asked the girl.

Uh-oh, I thought. *Her* name is Sunshine, too. I decided on the spot not to tell the new people about my nickname. In fact I decided not to talk to them at all. I was about to make a run for it when Sunshine and her mother saw me and said, "Hi."

"We're moving into this house," the woman added. She had the prettiest smile I'd ever seen. "I'm Betsy Winslow. This is Sunshine Daydream Winslow."

"But everybody calls me Sunny," the girl said. "What's your name?"

"Dawn," I replied. I pointed vaguely up the block. "I live around here." (I didn't want them to know exactly where I lived.)

"We came all the way from Oregon," Sunny told me.

"I know," I said without thinking. Before they could ask me how I knew, I added, "Do you need some help?"

"That would be wonderful," Mrs. Winslow said. "Could you carry this spider plant inside?"

"Spider plant?" I repeated in horror.

Sunny laughed. "It doesn't have spiders on it," she said. "It just looks like spiders." She held out the teapot planter her mother had handed her. I backed away just in case, but I could see what she meant. The leaves were grouped around the stem in a way that looked exactly like spider's legs.

The spider plants were just the first of the new and different things I saw the weekend the Winslows moved in. For example, instead of a living room couch they put huge pillows on the floor.

"Don't you need a couch to sit on when you watch TV?" I asked Sunny.

"We don't have a TV," she said happily. "TV rots your brain." She grabbed my hand and gave it a little tug. "Come on," she said. "We're having lunch."

On moving day most people get take-out to eat on the run. But not the Winslows. Mr.

Winslow had prepared a sit-down lunch. "Yummy," Sunny said as we entered the kitchen. "Kelp soup. My favorite."

"What's kelp?" I asked.

"Seaweed," said Sunny. "It's delicious."

"I have to go home for lunch," I mumbled.

As I ran out the back door I heard Mrs. Winslow say, "We thank the earth and sea for this meal."

I didn't tell my mother much about the new neighbors. But I thought about them as I ate a grilled cheese sandwich and tomato soup. What I was thinking was that I couldn't be friends with a girl as strange as Sunshine Daydream Winslow.

The next morning my mother asked me if I was going to invite "that new girl" to play.

"I don't know," I answered. "Maybe."

I watched a rerun of *Sesame Street* with Jeff. I wondered if Sunny thought *Sesame Street* rotted people's brains, too.

My mother came into the living room and turned off the TV. "You two get outside and play. It's a beautiful day."

I ambled out front and sat on the step. Jeff's friend Mark came over with two plastic swords. After a few minutes I decided that playing with the new girl couldn't be as boring as watching Jeff and Mark chase one another with fake swords.

The Winslows' kitchen door was open so I walked inside. No one was in the kitchen. I noticed a garden hose connected to the kitchen sink. I followed it up the stairs and into the master bedroom.

Sunny and her parents were squatting around what looked like a huge rubber raft. Sunny saw me first. "Hi," she said. "We're setting up Mom and Dad's waterbed."

Waterbed? Sunny's parents had a bed made of water? I'd never heard of such a thing. But Sunny seemed to accept it as a fact of life. I watched the rubber mattress expanding and wondered what it would be like to sleep on it.

"This is boring," Sunny said. "Wanna help me fix up my room?"

"Sure," I answered.

I was relieved to see that Sunny had a regular mattress, even if it was on the floor instead of up on a bedframe. Her bedspread was all different colors in a sloppy pattern.

"Isn't my bedspread pretty?" she said. "My mom and I made it. It's tie-dyed."

It didn't look to me as if it were made of dead ties, but I didn't say anything.

I helped Sunny tack up a poster next to her window. It was a big white dove on a blue background that said *Peace*. Then we hung up a huge, hand-painted cardboard rainbow over her bed. Those were the only things in her room so far. A mattress, a poster, and a cardboard rainbow. I looked around the room and asked, "Where are your toys?"

She dragged a moving box over to the mattress. "They're in here," she replied. We sat on the bed and unpacked the box. Sunny had a rag doll, a wooden whistle, a wooden train set, and some wooden blocks. I could appreciate the blocks, but I'd outgrown them *years* earlier. Poor Sunny, I thought, these toys are pathetic.

"Don't you have a Barbie Doll or anything?" I asked.

"We try not to buy plastic or other synthetics," she said. "They're not good for the environment."

At that point I hadn't thought much about saving the environment. And I certainly didn't know what a "synthetic" was. To me it sounded like a disease.

"Can you play with plastic if it's other people's toys?" I asked.

"I guess," she replied. "But I like my toys. Hey, you haven't met Captain. He's my most special." Sunny reached under her pillow and pulled out a mangy-looking, pea green, stuffed animal.

I tried to hide my disgust by asking, "What is it?"

"A crocodile," she said as she hugged the ratty thing.

Sunny probably could tell I was bored with her toys. "I know what we can do," she said. "Let's play with Morse Code."

"Who's that?"

She giggled. "Morse Code isn't a person. It's a way of communicating, like a secret language. My mom and I use it all the time. Here, I'll show you." She picked up two wooden blocks and hit them together several times. She sounded like a drummer who couldn't find the beat. When she stopped she said, "I just spoke to you in Morse Code."

"What'd you say?" I asked.

" 'Hi, Dawn.' "

"It took a long time to say that," I commented.

"That's because there's long and short bangs for every letter," she said. "I'll show you."

Sunny opened a notebook and handed me a sheet of paper. On it was a list of the letters of the alphabet. After each letter were dots and dashes. "See," she said, "you can write in Morse Code, too." Sunny happily chattered on about Morse Code. I wasn't even close to being interested, but I had good enough manners to pretend I was paying attention.

Then Sunny went to the door of her room. "Look at the chart," she said, "and see if you can figure out what I'm saying." She hit those old blocks against one another again. I tried to follow, but not very hard.

When she finally stopped banging I asked, "What'd you say?"

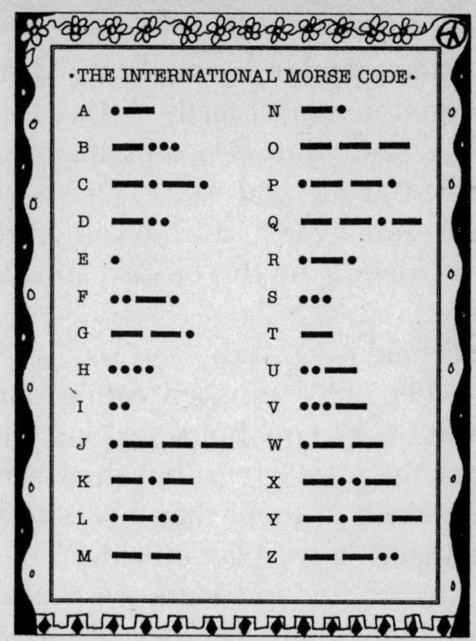

·THE INTERNATIONAL MORSE CODE·

| | | | |
|---|---|---|---|
| A | •— | N | —• |
| B | —••• | O | ——— |
| C | —•—• | P | •——• |
| D | —•• | Q | ——•— |
| E | • | R | •—• |
| F | ••—• | S | ••• |
| G | ——• | T | — |
| H | •••• | U | ••— |
| I | •• | V | •••— |
| J | •——— | W | •—— |
| K | —•— | X | —••— |
| L | •—•• | Y | —•—— |
| M | —— | Z | ——•• |

Sunny's secret language.

"You'll see," she said. "Just wait. It'll come through the door."

While we waited for something to "come through the door" Sunny said, "Don't feel bad because you didn't get it. It takes time to learn Morse Code. We'll practice all summer. Then when school starts we'll have a secret language."

I thought, she's crazy if she thinks I'll go around school banging blocks together!

Sunny's mother entered the room then and handed each of us an apple. "Here you are, girls," she said.

"Tell Dawn how you knew we wanted apples," Sunny said.

"She asked in Morse Code," her mother answered matter-of-factly. I have to confess that I was pretty impressed by that. Mrs. Winslow smiled at me and said, "Dawn, your mother just came over to introduce herself. Everyone is so friendly on this block. I already love living here."

"Thanks," I said.

When we'd finished eating our apples we went over to my house to play. Sunny looked at all my plastic toys, but she wasn't any more interested in them than I was in her toys. So I suggested we play outside.

My brother and Mark were still in the front yard with their swords. "They shouldn't be playing like that," Sunny said.

I thought she meant because the swords were plastic. But she had another complaint. "Playing with swords is like playing with toy guns," she said. "It encourages violence. We have to stop them by suggesting a peaceful game."

In a few minutes I was playing statues with Sunny, Jeff, and Mark. I had wanted a friend my age on the block so I wouldn't have to play with three- and four-year-olds!

Finally it was time for Sunny to go home. Before she left she thrust a folded piece of paper into my hand. "This is for you," she said. "It's my Morse Code chart. You can have it. I already know it by heart."

I took the paper even though I wasn't planning on learning Morse Code.

"Let's play together tomorrow, too," Sunny added.

"Sure," I said. "See you tomorrow."

The next morning, before I even had a chance to figure out if I wanted to play with Sunshine Daydream Winslow, she was knocking at our kitchen door.

"Hi, Sunny," my mother said. "Come on in."

Sunny sat across from me while I finished my cereal. "Wait till you see what my mom's doing," she said. "She said we could help." Sunny told me that her mother was tie-dyeing some fabric to make into curtains for their new house. This time I asked what tie-dye was.

"You tie cloth in little bunches with rubber bands," Sunny explained. "Then you put it in dye, any color you want. Sometimes you use more than one color. When you take off the rubber bands it makes neat patterns like this." She pointed to a blotchy round shape on her T-shirt. "I made this myself," she bragged.

I didn't think her T-shirt was very pretty, but I was interested enough in tie-dyeing to want to try it. Especially when my mother said I could tie-dye one of my white T-shirts.

By the time we were walking over to Sunny's house I was downright enthusiastic about tie-dyeing. Then I saw that Mrs. Winslow had set up two big tubs in the front yard. The tie-dyeing was going to happen right in the front yard.

Sunny ran to the tubs and looked inside. "Purple and yellow," she called to me. "I love it when we use purple." Sunny ran back to me and grabbed my hand. "Come on," she said. "Let's help."

Mrs. Winslow was sitting on the grass with a pile of white cloth on her lap. She looked as if she were doing her laundry on the front lawn. I also noticed that Mr. Winslow was digging a big circle in the front lawn. "What's your dad doing?" I asked Sunny.

"He's going to plant white flowers in the shape of a peace symbol," she replied. "Isn't that great?"

"Yeah," I said. "Great."

I noticed that Mrs. Stevenson, whose house was across the street from the Winslows', was staring at us through her picture window. And that Mr. Landers slowed his car down as he drove by.

I patted my stomach as if I had a stomachache. "I don't feel so good," I told Sunny. "I must have eaten too much. I've got to go home. I'll tie-dye some other time."

I could see that Sunny was disappointed. "Do you want me to do your T-shirt for you?" she asked.

"Nah," I said. "That's okay."

As I walked home I felt a little guilty about saying I'd do something and then making up an excuse for not doing it. But I figured Sunny Winslow probably didn't care. When I was gone she could tie-dye cloth in metal tubs with her mother and plant flowers with her father while the neighbors watched. Sunny Winslow's idea of fun.

By the time I went to bed that night I'd made up my mind that Sunny and her family were just too weird for me. I was disappointed that the only girl on the block who was my age wasn't going to be my friend.

The next morning my mother asked me if I was going to play with Sunny Winslow. "No," I said. "I'm a little tired." I faked a yawn.

"Her mother was saying how nicely you two play together."

"Uh-huh," I said. I turned back to my coloring book.

A little later my mother returned to my room. "Well, it's settled," she said. "We're taking Betsy and Sunny Winslow shopping."

"How come?" I asked.

"Betsy doesn't have her car today and she needs some things for the house. I'll drive us over to Bamberger's department store. Jeff is playing at Mark's house this afternoon, so we'll have a girls' day out."

I couldn't believe my bad luck. My mother was becoming friends with Sunny's mother! It was going to be harder than I thought to avoid Sunny.

I didn't say too much in the car as we drove to Bamberger's. My mom and Sunny's mom chattered away about tofu recipes and the great California weather. Sunny hummed a song about peace and love. I looked out the window and wished that Sunny and her mother weren't wearing their nightgown-dresses.

Sunny pointed to the sky. "Look at the clouds," she said. "They're stratus clouds. We're going to have a thunderstorm for sure."

By the time we parked in the Bamberger's lot I heard a distant roll of thunder. I figured Sunny had heard a weather forecast before she left home.

We followed our mothers around the housewares department for awhile. I hated how people stared at us. Sunny and her mother looked so weird with their long hair and hippie clothes. Suddenly, I got an idea for how I could shake Sunny. "Mom, can we check out the toy department while you guys shop?" I asked.

A minute later my mother and Mrs. Winslow rode with us on the elevator to the sixth floor toy department. "Remember, we'll be on the second floor in housewares," my mother said.

"And we'll come back up here for you in twenty minutes," Mrs. Winslow reminded us.

Once our mothers were gone I headed for the Barbie Doll section and started looking at all the plastic stuff you could buy for her, such as a house and furniture. I figured Sunny would be so disgusted that she'd look for toys that were made of wood. But she followed me and kept talking about how the dumps of the world were filling up with plastic and that plastic would never turn into soil like other garbage. The toy department was very crowded and it seemed to me that everyone going up and down our aisle stared at us.

I just kept looking at one toy after another — all of them plastic — and pretended I didn't know the girl in the long skirt who was lecturing about garbage. Maybe that's why I didn't notice that a terrible storm had started.

"It's a big storm," Sunny said.

"If it's such a big store," I replied, "why don't you go look for some toys that aren't plastic?"

"I said, 'It's a big *storm,*' " Sunny replied with a giggle. "Not *'store.'* "

"Oh," I said.

Finally Sunny wandered off to another aisle. She'd only been gone a minute when I heard a tremendous clap of thunder. The store lights flickered — and went out. I was in total darkness.

I heard people shout, "Oh-hh," and "I can't see a thing." I felt frightened. I wanted my mother. But how would I ever find her in the dark? I took a few steps forward and bumped into a display case. I would have started crying then if Sunny hadn't called out, "Dawn, stay where you are. I'll find you."

"Okay," I answered in a trembling voice.

I soon saw a flicker of red and yellow light coming toward me. Sunny was carrying a big toy clown with a lit-up nose. She was using the clown like a flashlight. Sunny took my hand. "Come on," she said. "Let's find a salesclerk and tell her that our mothers are on the second floor."

All around us, in the pitch dark, I could hear customers grumbling. A child was crying. But when people saw Sunny and me with our clown light, they relaxed and laughed a little.

"Well, look at that," a man said. "Isn't that clever."

A woman said, "See, Jaimie, you don't have to be afraid. Those girls aren't."

Finally our clown nose shone on a woman dressed in the blue Bamberger's jacket.

"We're all by ourselves," Sunny explained. "Our mothers are on the second floor in housewares. They were going to come get us."

Just then the electricity came back on. Everyone blinked at the bright store lights. Some people cheered.

"Well," the clerk said. "I guess your moms will be able to find you now. Meanwhile I'll keep an eye on you. My name is Mrs. Stazio."

During the next few minutes a lot of the shoppers left. I guess they were afraid the electricity might go out again. I know I was. I decided to stick close to Sunny. We cruised the aisles looking for more light-up toys, just in case. After awhile, Sunny said we should check in with Mrs. Stazio.

"You've been waiting for a pretty long time," Mrs. Stazio said. "Let's go down to housewares and see if your mothers are there."

Sunny pointed to another clerk in the toy department. "Let's tell him where we're going in case our moms come up here when we're downstairs."

Mrs. Stazio patted Sunny on the head. "Good thinking," she said. "If I ever got marooned on a desert island I'd want you along."

We took the stairs down to the second floor. "We don't want to be in an elevator if the electricity goes out again," Mrs. Stazio explained. I noticed she was carrying a Batman flashlight.

The three of us walked up and down the housewares aisles. When we didn't find our mothers we questioned the clerks in that department. One of them remembered a "pretty hippie lady in a long skirt who bought wooden spoons," but she hadn't seen her since the lights went on.

"The next step is to make an announcement over the P.A. system," Mrs. Stazio said.

I was feeling scared and had to swallow tears. But Sunny remained calm.

A few minutes later we heard: "Two girls are waiting for their mothers at the cashier's desk in housewares."

I gulped. I couldn't wait to see my mother again. I knew that when she hugged me and said how worried she'd been I would cry and cry. But where was she?

Sunny, meanwhile, was looking around thoughtfully. "Who are those men?" she asked Mrs. Stazio.

I looked where Sunny was pointing and saw two men in blue workmen's overalls. One carried a big tool box. The other had slung a heavy duty extension cord over his shoulder.

"They're from the elevator repair company," Mrs. Stazio said. "Maybe an elevator's stuck."

"If there's a stuck elevator," Sunny said, "I bet our mothers are in it."

"That certainly would explain where they've been," Mrs. Stazio said. "Let's go find out."

My mother stuck in an elevator! What if there wasn't enough air in there? What if the elevator plunged to the ground and everyone was crushed? What if one of the people stuck with my mother was a murderer?

We caught up with the repairmen. "Hey, fellows," Mrs. Stazio said, "what's going on here?"

"Stuck elevator," one of them answered.

"Must have happened because of the power failure."

"Is anyone in it?" Sunny asked.

"Suppose so," the man said. "Store's pretty busy today." He pounded on the door and shouted, "Hey! Anybody in there?"

We heard an answering bang from inside the wall. There were people in the stuck elevator!

"Is everyone all right in there?" the repairman shouted. We listened. No answer. "They can't hear my voice," the repairman said. "Just the pounding."

Sunny approached the repairman and said something to him. Then she started pounding on the elevator door herself.

"What's she doing?" Mrs. Stazio asked in alarm.

At first I thought Sunny had gone mad. Then I figured it out. "It's Morse code," I told Mrs. Stazio. "If Sunny's mom is on the elevator she'll understand it."

When Sunny finished pounding we heard knocks inside the wall. Through Morse code we learned that there were five people on the elevator, including our moms. No one was sick or injured, and they were stuck between the second and third floors. The repairman then told Sunny to ask her mother some questions, such as if a certain light was on in the elevator car. With information from inside the elevator the repairman said they'd be able to do the repair work twice as fast. With a little luck our mothers would be free within an hour.

A group of shoppers were now standing around the elevator watching Sunny pounding out Morse code with her fist. "Isn't that something," I heard someone say. "A little kid like that knowing Morse code." I didn't hear one person say she looked strange in a long skirt. I was proud to know Sunny. And thanks to her I wasn't frightened anymore. I knew my mother would be okay. Finally I was calm enough to think of what I could do to help.

"I need to use a phone," I told Mrs. Stazio. "To call my dad."

I phoned my father at work and told him what had happened. "I'll be right there," he said.

"First call Mr. Winslow," I told him. "He works at the social services office in Palo City. And you should call Mark's parents and see if Jeff can stay there longer."

"Good thinking, Sunshine," my dad said. "I'm proud of you."

My dad and Mr. Winslow had arrived at Bamberger's by the time the elevator doors opened and five weary people walked out.

Sunny and I ran to our mothers.

"Are you okay?" I asked Mom when we were finished hugging.

"I'm fine," she said. "I'd have been really frightened if it hadn't been for Betsy. She was as calm and sensible as anyone could be in an emergency."

Just like Sunny, I thought.

The other three people on the elevator wanted to meet Sunny and thank her for her help. The elevator repairmen said she could come work for them anytime. The store manager shook Sunny's hand and thanked her personally. She invited our families and the other people who had been stuck in the elevator to go to Bamberger's cafeteria and have something to eat. "It'll be on the house," she said.

Our parents thanked her and decided that we'd go to the cafeteria for an early supper.

"The cafeteria is on the fourth floor," my mother said.

"Let's take the stairs," Mrs. Winslow said.

We all laughed — and took the stairs.

Sunny and I made sure to sit next to one another in the cafeteria. And we both ordered the same thing, chicken tacos and lemonade.

When it was time to leave, Sunny and I said we wanted to ride home together.

"Let's go in my car," Sunny said.

*Sunshine Daydream Winslow and me.*
*I never thought we'd become best friends.*

I thought of the Winslows' silly-looking flower car. Did I want to be seen getting out of that car? Then I realized that I didn't care anymore what other people thought of the Winslows. I liked my new neighbors.

"Sure," I said. "Let's go in your car." As we bumped up our street in the Winslows' little car I felt lucky that I had a good friend who lived on my block. In fact I was beginning to think that Sunshine Daydream Winslow was just about the most interesting, smart, resourceful girl I'd ever met. Maybe we would be best friends after all.

# The Golden Anniversary

I was a happy ten-year-old. I loved where I lived and had a best friend just two houses away. School was great and so was life at home. My brother and I had parents who loved one another and loved us. I was on top of the world.

# The Golden Anniversary

By fifth grade, Jill, Maggie, Sunny, and I were very best friends. Don't think we were one of those obnoxious cliques, though. We played with other kids, too. It's just that everyone knew that we were special friends.

My parents and Sunny's parents were also good friends. Mr. and Mrs. Winslow weren't as hippie-ish as they had been when they moved to our block. The flowerbed peace symbol on their front lawn was gone. Now their lawn was a field of wildflowers. It was neat to have one lawn on the block that wasn't mowed down to within an inch of its life. And when the Winslows got a new car they didn't paint flowers on it.

Our families had some great times together. I especially remember one evening picnic on the beach. We swam in the ocean as the sun was setting. Then we ate a supper of salads, Mrs. Winslow's home-baked bread, fruit, and cookies. After supper we lay on the beach and looked at the stars. Sunny and her parents knew all the constellations. My dad and mom knew some, too. They were saying where and when they'd learned about the stars.

"Did you ever wonder what's pouring out of the Big Dipper?" Sunny asked me.

"I know," Jeff said. "Green slime."

Sunny and I ignored his answer. "Maybe meteors," I said.

"I think it's pouring out love," Sunny said.

I noticed my dad had put his arm around my mom and she had rested her head on his shoulder.

My mom looked in my direction and said, "Come sit with us, sweetie."

I leaned against them. Just then a falling star streaked downward across the sky. And we all saw it.

As we were packing up to go home, my mother said, "My parents are having their fiftieth wedding anniversary next month."

"Granny and Pop-Pop?" I asked.

"Yup. We haven't seen them in a long time. I think their golden wedding anniversary is a perfect time to do something about that."

Because my grandparents lived across the country in Connecticut we didn't see them as much as we wanted to. So I was pretty excited to think I'd be seeing them soon.

On the way home we thought about what we could do to make Granny's and Pop-Pop's anniversary special. Dad suggested we fly to Connecticut and give a special dinner party for them and their friends. But Mom, who's not the most organized person in the world, said it would be difficult to plan a party long-distance.

Then Mom suggested we treat Granny and Pop-Pop to a vacation weekend that would be extra special because we'd go, too. Dad thought that was a terrific idea. "Tomorrow night at dinner we'll talk about where to go," Mom said.

The next night, Jeff announced, "I know where to go for Granny and Pop-Pop's anniversary. A dude ranch in Colorado. That'd be great!"

"Granny and Pop-Pop are almost eighty years old," my mother reminded him. "And neither of them has ever been interested in horseback riding."

"Well, here's my idea," I said. "I think we should go to a fancy beach resort, like in the Caribbean. Maggie and her parents do that all the time."

"That's not Granny and Pop-Pop's sort of thing, either," my mom said.

"Okay," I went on, "here's another idea. We could go to New York City! We could visit the Statue of Liberty and the Empire State Building. And go to a Broadway show."

"And we can go to a basketball game in Madison Square Garden," Jeff added. "That's even better than a dude ranch."

"Hold it, kids," my dad said. "Two things. First of all, you are thinking of things *you'd* like to do instead of what Granny and Pop-Pop might like to do. Secondly, since they live near New York City they've been going there on special occasions all their lives."

I realized then that Granny's and Pop-Pop's anniversary vacation would take some serious thinking and planning. After dinner I scooted upstairs and found my atlas. We were studying the map of the United States and talking about all the places we might go to when a horrible thought came to me. "What if Granny and Pop-Pop have already planned something for their anniversary?" I asked.

A look of panic crossed my mother's face. "We'd better reserve that weekend right now," she said. "We'll call them. But Jeff and Dawn, let me tell them, okay?" We each went to an extension phone so everybody could talk.

Granny and Pop-Pop asked us lots of questions about school and what we'd been doing. They told us how lousy the February weather was in Stoneybrook and we told them how great the weather was in Palo City. Jeff kept interrupting to ask stupid knock-knock jokes. With Jeff and me yakking away to our grandparents, my mother couldn't fit a word in edgewise.

Suddenly Mom shouted, "Knock knock."

Everyone laughed because my mother hates knock-knock jokes.

"Who's there?" we all replied.

"Fiftieth," Mom answered.

"Fiftieth who?"

"Fiftieth wedding anniversary and we're all going to celebrate it together," she announced.

Granny and Pop-Pop laughed.

"That's not a joke, Mom," Jeff complained.

"It isn't a joke," my mother agreed. "It's an invitation." Then my mother told Granny and Pop-Pop to keep their wedding anniversary weekend open because they were going to spend it with us.

"Oh, you're coming here, dear," Granny said. "That's wonderful."

"No, we're not," Jeff said. "You're going to meet us someplace, but we don't know where yet."

"Further details will come in the mail," my mom said.

When we'd hung up the phones and met back in the kitchen Mom was singing, " 'San Francisco, open your Golden Gate . . .' "

"San Francisco!" my father exclaimed.

"That's perfect. The city of the *Golden* Gate Bridge for a *golden* wedding anniversary."

"I'll order the plane tickets tomorrow," my mother said.

The next day my mom and I went to the bookstore and bought a book about San Francisco. Jeff and I poured through the book and made a list of what we wanted to do there. San Francisco was a great city! We were going to have a ball.

- Cable car tour
- Hike along Golden Gate Promenade (3 miles)
- Hike over Golden Gate Bridge (2 miles)
- Steinhart Aquarium
- San Francisco Zoo
- Filbert steps (with 377 steps to climb)
- Climb all 42 hills
- Fort Funston (walk down cliff to beach)
- Fisherman's Wharf
- Chinatown

We showed the list to my mother. "A three-mile hike along a promenade and a two-mile walk across the bridge!" she exclaimed. "The aquarium *and* the zoo. And what's this? Filbert!" She looked at us and smiled patiently. "Have you forgotten that your grandparents are elderly? I expect they'll be a lot frailer than the last time we saw them."

"Can't we do *any* of these things?" I asked plaintively.

"Of course you can," she answered. "But don't plan anything too strenuous and leave time for Granny and Pop-Pop to take naps in the afternoon."

Even though I was disappointed, I made up my mind that we'd still have fun. With my mother's help, Jeff and I cut down our list of San Francisco tourist activities by quite a bit. For example, we'd skip climbing down the cliffs to the beach and instead of walking across the Golden Gate Bridge we'd take a bus.

A few weeks later we boarded a plane for San Francisco. I thought I was going to burst I was so excited. During the flight my mother said, "Granny and Pop-Pop's plane is scheduled to land half an hour after ours." She sighed. "Poor things. I hope they're not too wiped out by the long plane ride."

As soon as we got off our plane we checked arrivals and departures for United flight #567 from Connecticut. While we waited at Gate 12, I imagined my old, frail grandparents tottering off the plane. I thought, I'll have to take especially good care of them. I'll make sure they hold on to me when they walk through the airport. I didn't want them knocked over by rushing travelers.

My dad pointed and waved. "Look, kids," he said. "There they are!"

"Mom, Dad!" my mother called. "Over here."

Granny and Pop-Pop broke away from the stream of people rushing through the gate and ran to us.

"Hey, hey," Pop-Pop said as he lifted Jeff into the air. "There's our boy." He put Jeff down and wrapped me in a big bear hug. "And our girl. Dawn, I've missed you."

My mother and grandmother were hugging like crazy. "Mother," my mom cried, "I've missed you so much."

"I know, I know," Granny said. "I've missed you, too." Granny and my mother were crying. And so was I. I noticed that my dad and Pop-Pop had tears in their eyes, too.

"Why's everybody crying?" Jeff asked.

"Enough tears," Pop-Pop said. He held up a guidebook to San Francisco. It was the one that Jeff and I had been using to make our lists! "There's a whole bunch of things to do in this town and I intend to do them all, hills included. How about the rest of you?"

We cheered.

"Mom said you were too old to walk across the Golden Gate Bridge," Jeff said.

"Tell your mother I'll *race* her across the Golden Gate Bridge," Pop-Pop replied.

We laughed and hugged all over again.

When we arrived at our hotel and were settled in our rooms on the seventeenth floor, my mom and dad suggested we have dinner in a nearby restaurant. They thought that would be best for Granny and Pop-Pop after their long flight. But Granny said, "Oh, let's go to Chinatown instead. It's supposed to be a great place to walk around. I could use some exercise after sitting all day on that plane."

We had fun walking around Chinatown. We checked out the shops that spilled out onto the street and ate the most delicious Chinese food I'd ever had.

After dinner we walked back to the hotel. Mom and Dad were holding hands. I was surprised that Granny and Pop-Pop didn't walk together, too. Instead Granny was walking with Jeff and Pop-Pop was walking with me.

The plan the next morning was to meet Granny and Pop-Pop in the hotel dining room for breakfast at eight o'clock. Since I was the first Schafer to be ready, I took the elevator to the lobby and went to the restaurant by myself. My grandparents were already there. They had spread maps of San Francisco and the guidebook on the table in front of them. They were so engrossed in making plans for the day that they didn't notice me.

"Well, if you want to go look at fish, dear, you just go ahead and look at the fish," Granny was saying. "This is my one opportunity to see the flowers at Golden Gate Park and I intend to see them and take photographs of them for my garden club."

"After the aquarium I may just take me to the Ansel Adams Center and see some *good* photographs," Pop-Pop said.

"Some people look at pictures and some people take them," Granny shot back.

She looked up then and saw me. " 'Morning, sweetie," she said as she opened her arms for a good morning hug.

When we were all seated at the table and had ordered breakfast, Granny announced, "There's so much to do in San Francisco I think that after we take the trolley car tour this morning we should split up."

My mother agreed. "We could see a lot more that way. And we'll be together tonight for dinner."

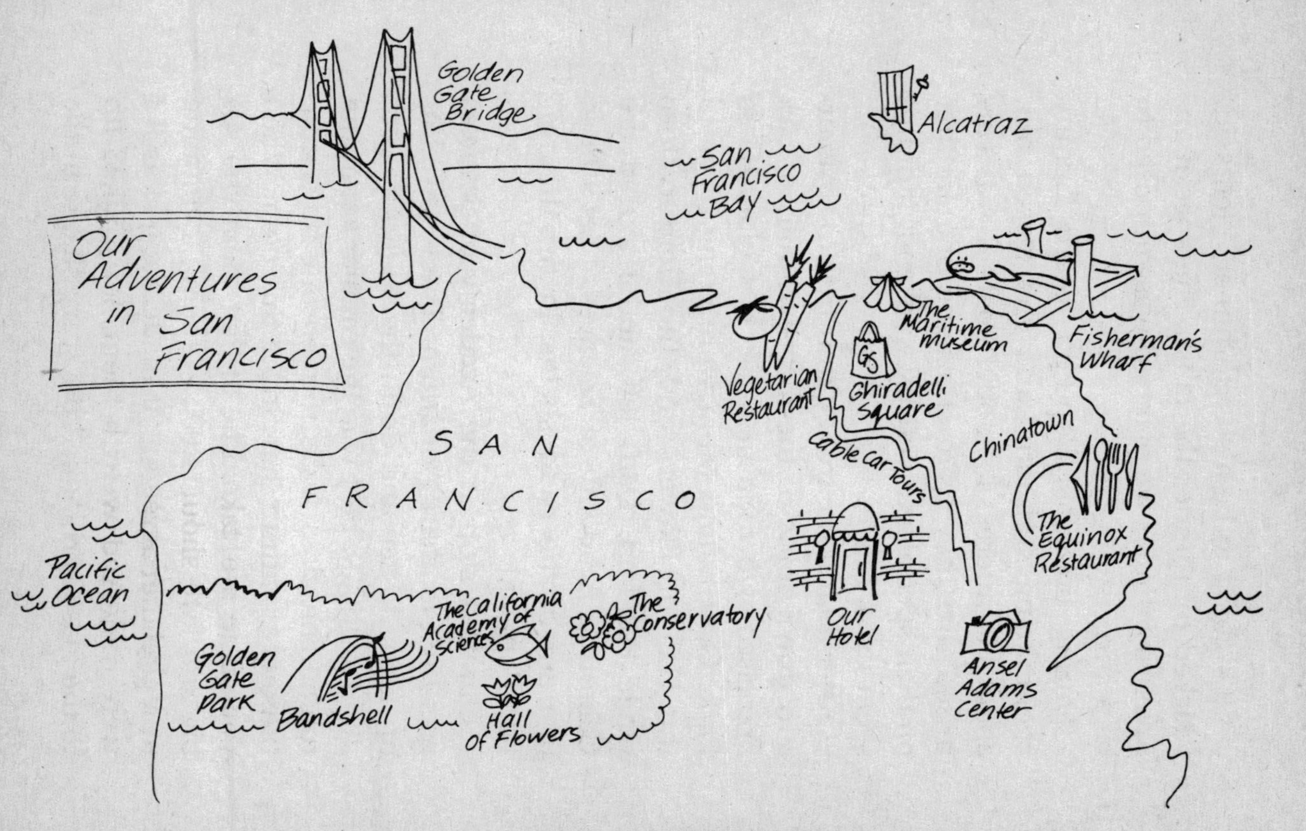
Our Adventures in San Francisco
Golden Gate Bridge
Alcatraz
San Francisco Bay
Vegetarian Restaurant
The Maritime Museum
Fisherman's Wharf
Ghiradelli Square
Chinatown
Cable Car Tours
The Equinox Restaurant
SAN FRANCISCO
Pacific Ocean
Our Hotel
Ansel Adams Center
The California Academy of Sciences
The Conservatory
Golden Gate Park
Bandshell
Hall of Flowers
What a weekend!

"It's going to be a *special* dinner," Jeff said. I kicked him under the table. The special anniversary dinner we planned was supposed to be a surprise.

During breakfast Pop-Pop teased Granny about being stubborn, and she teased him about his interest in model boats. I was surprised that they were criticizing one another on their special anniversary weekend. It didn't seem right.

After a fantastic trolley tour that took us up and down some of the forty-two hills of San Francisco, we rode in a cab to Golden Gate Park. Granny and Mom were going to go to the Hall of Flowers and the Conservatory while Pop-Pop, Dad, Jeff, and I toured the California Academy of Sciences. "Let's meet in front of the band shelter in two hours," Pop-Pop said.

Our first stop at the Academy of Sciences was the Steinhart Aquarium. There were lots of things to see and do in the aquarium, but the part I liked best was the circular aquarium room. The glass walls formed one huge continuous aquarium that circled the room. When you stand in the middle of that room you see big and little fish (14,000 of them!) swimming in a circle around you. It made me feel as if I were under water with them. We walked up to the glass and looked big scary sharks in the eye. I'd never seen deep-sea fish so close up before. Or since.

When we left the aquarium we went to the Space and Earth Hall. The neatest thing there was the earthquake floor. If that's what a real earthquake feels like I never want to be in one.

At one o'clock we met Granny and Mom in front of the band shelter. We sat on the grass and drank lemonade and talked about what we wanted to do at our next stop, Fisherman's Wharf. Mom and I were interested in shopping at the great malls on the wharf, such as Pier 39, the Cannery, and Ghirardelli Square. The guidebook said that these places were not only great for the stores and restaurants, but they were also very interesting buildings architecturally. "Let's have lunch at the vegetarian restaurant in Ghirardelli Square," my mom suggested. "It got a good write-up in the guidebook."

"Vegetables?" Pop-Pop said. "No broccoli and carrots for me! I want to eat fish at one of those outdoor spots on the pier. And I'm not going into any stores when it's so beautiful out."

"It looks like it's time to split up again," Granny said in a huff.

By the time we reached Fisherman's Wharf we'd decided that Granny, Mom, and I would have lunch at Ghirardelli Square and spend the rest of the afternoon in the malls. The guys would eat fish on the pier and go to the Maritime Museum.

At the wharf Mom reminded us, "Don't forget that we're eating at the Equinox restaurant tonight. It's at the top of the Hyatt Regency Hotel. Let's meet in the main lobby at seven-thirty." She winked at me. We had the most wonderful anniversary dinner planned for Granny and Pop-Pop.

Mom and Dad kissed good-bye then, but not Granny and Pop-Pop. They were still sniping at one another. Pop-Pop said, "Watch your step, old lady, and don't spend all your money in one place."

Granny told him, "Don't expect me to take care of you if you get sick from eating raw oysters."

I hated hearing them talk like that. Weren't they supposed to be the happy fiftieth-wedding-anniversary couple?

My mother didn't seem to notice. As we walked down the street together she put one arm around me and the other around Granny. "The two women I love most in the world," she said. "I couldn't be happier."

Before we went into Ghirardelli Square we walked along the wharf. Hundreds of sea lions had taken over two piers. It wasn't a zoo, just a natural occurrence. The sea lions were cute,

*Me at Fisherman's Wharf with a bunch of sea lions.*

loud, and funny. Granny took my picture near them.

The restaurant Mom picked for us served fabulous vegetarian food. I ordered a cheese burrito, guacamole, and a salad with about ten different kinds of lettuce in it. Our table was on a terrace overlooking the bay. Granny couldn't get over the fact that she was eating outdoors in March.

After lunch we shopped. I bought bookends (wooden) for Sunny that were shaped and painted like rainbows. Mom bought me a T-shirt with a picture of the Golden Gate Bridge on the front and *I ♥ San Francisco* on the back. Then we helped Granny pick out a dress. She tried on several. But we agreed that a royal blue silk dress looked best on her. "It's beautiful, Mother," my mom told Granny. "You should buy it and wear it to dinner tonight."

"I will," Granny said. "I'll call it my anniversary dress. Fifty years married to Charlie, I deserve something."

Mom laughed at that. But I thought it was sad. I'd always thought my grandparents were happily married. But then, since I live in California and they live in Connecticut, I don't spend much time with them. I knew that I loved them both very much. What I hadn't known was that they didn't love one another. And they'd spent fifty years together, five times my whole life. How awful to spend fifty years with someone you didn't love!

As we walked away from Fisherman's Wharf and up another one of the forty-two hills, I compared Granny and Pop-Pop to my parents. I remembered the way my mother and father had walked hand in hand the night before. How they kissed good-bye when we broke into two groups at the Fisherman's Wharf. I just knew that my parents would still be madly in love when they celebrated their fiftieth wedding anniversary.

# CHAPTER 8

Granny, Mom, and I returned to our hotel rooms to dress for dinner. While Mom and I were alone in our rooms, she telephoned the restaurant to be sure our table was set up just the way we wanted it.

Granny looked beautiful in her new dress. I had a feeling she guessed that we were planning a surprise. As we were leaving our hotel we met Dad and Jeff coming in. They'd decided to freshen up and change for the special dinner, too.

"Where's Dad?" my mother asked.

"He didn't want to bother coming back to the hotel," my father answered.

"He's walking," Jeff added. "He likes hills. He's going to meet us at the restaurant."

"Charlie has always loved wandering around alone in strange cities," Granny said.

I was disappointed that Pop-Pop wasn't going to dress up for his anniversary dinner.

When I whispered that to my mom, she reminded me that Pop-Pop didn't know it was a special dinner.

We waited for Jeff and my dad to dress and then we took a cab to the Hyatt Regency Hotel. We arrived there at seven-thirty on the dot. "Charlie's probably waiting for us," Granny said as we walked into the hotel lobby. "One thing I can say for him, he's punctual."

But Pop-Pop wasn't waiting for us. Mom went up to the restaurant in case he was waiting for us there. The rest of us sat on a couch and a couple of chairs with a view of the front entrance to the hotel. When Mom returned Pop-Pop wasn't with her.

Jeff, Mom, Dad, and I talked about what we'd done during the afternoon. But Granny didn't say anything. She concentrated on watching the front doors for Pop-Pop. During the next ten minutes they opened several times. But no Pop-Pop.

Finally Granny said something. "How many oysters did he eat?" she asked my dad.

"Two dozen. But so did I."

"Two dozen!" Granny repeated. "Mercy. He must have gotten sick. And all by himself in a strange city." Her eyes filled with tears.

My mother told Granny that she was sure Pop-Pop was okay. That he probably was distracted by some interesting tourist attraction.

Or maybe he was a little lost. "But he'll show up here sooner or later," she assured Granny. "Pop knows how to take care of himself."

"You don't understand," Granny said. "When your father and I travel we often split up. As we did today. Then we meet for dinner. Also as we did today. But not once in fifty years of marriage has Charlie Porter been late for one of those meetings. In fact, he's always at the restaurant when I arrive. He doesn't want me to worry."

"Maybe he went to the wrong restaurant," I said. I looked through our trusty travel guide to see if there was another restaurant called Equinox, or anything that sounded like it. There wasn't. Meanwhile Mom phoned our hotel to see if Pop-Pop was there or had been. He hadn't.

At 7:50 I heard Granny whisper to my mother, "At eight o'clock we'll call the police and check the hospitals."

But she didn't have to. The next time the lobby doors opened, Pop-Pop walked in. Jeff shouted, "There he is!" Everyone in the lobby stared at us. Boy, did we ever give them a show! We ran to Pop-Pop. "What a welcome," he exclaimed. Then he saw that Granny was crying.

"Oh, my darling," he said in a voice that was both sad and frightened. "What is it?

What's wrong?" He enveloped her in his arms and she whispered into his ear. It was such a private, beautiful moment that the rest of us backed away a little.

After comforting Granny, Pop-Pop finally looked at us. "Which one of you told me dinner was at eight?" he asked.

"Uh-oh," Jeff said. He glanced at me. "Dawn, you said we'd have a special dinner at *eight*. You did."

"I also said that we were meeting at seven-thirty, goofy," I told him.

"Don't worry about it, Jeff," Pop-Pop said. "Just a little mix-up."

"Well, it's eight o'clock now," Dad said. He stood tall and said in a formal voice, "Ladies and gentlemen, please follow me."

We took the express elevator to the eighteenth floor. Mom told the reservation clerk that we were the Schafer party. A maître d' in a black tuxedo approached our group and said, "Ladies and gentlemen, please follow me." I had to hold my breath to keep from laughing out loud.

As we followed the maître d' into the fancy dining room I noticed that my grandparents were holding hands.

Our big round table was absolutely gorgeous. A low bouquet of Granny's favorite flowers was in the middle. A balloon was tied

The bride and groom--
fifty years later.

to the back of each of our chairs. The dishes, white with gold trim, looked like clouds on the soft blue tablecloth. At each place was a fancy printed menu. I read: "Fiftieth Wedding Anniversary Dinner Honoring Rita and Charles Porter." The four courses of our extra-special dinner were listed underneath. We had a choice of three dishes for each course.

We'd barely sat down when Jeff grabbed the table and whispered hoarsely, "The room's moving. It's an earthquake!"

We all laughed. I put my arm around him. "It's not an earthquake. This is a revolving dining room." I explained. "The room turns so we can see all of San Francisco through the windows while we're eating. It happens so slowly that you can hardly feel it."

"I feel it," Jeff said. He was still nervous.

When I pointed out that no one else in the restaurant was acting as though this were an earthquake he finally relaxed. "Oh, neato," Jeff said with relief.

The revolving restaurant was "neato." The whole evening was "neato." Between appetizers (I had stuffed mushrooms) and the main course (I ordered chicken divan) we gave Granny and Pop-Pop presents. Jeff's and my presents were individual school pictures in gold frames. "When we send our pictures next year you can change the picture and use the same frame," I explained.

"Neato," Granny said with a grin.

My parents' present was the trip to San Francisco and Saturday matinee ticket series to the Metropolitan Opera in New York City. "What a perfect gift," Granny said. "Going to the opera and the ballet are things that we both like to do."

"I suppose you're going to drive me crazy humming all those arias," Pop-Pop teased her. I was beginning to see that the way they were treating one another was loving teasing. Especially when Granny shot back, "My singing's a lot better than your imitations of the ballerinas we saw last month."

Pop-Pop winked at me and whispered, "The old girl's got a point."

I was wondering if my grandparents had gotten one another anniversary presents when Granny reached into her purse and pulled out a small square box, gift-wrapped in gold paper and tied with a gold ribbon. "I should have given you this present before," she told Pop-Pop when she handed it to him. "You could have used it."

Pop-Pop opened the package and took out a gold watch. "Put on your reading glasses and take a look at the back," Granny said.

He turned the watch over. "Don't need

glasses to read this, my dear," he said.

"What does it say?" I asked.

Pop-Pop didn't hear me. He was too busy kissing Granny thank you. I turned the watch over and read it myself. "C.T.P. & R.R.P. Time passes. Our love endures."

"Did you get Granny a present?" Jeff asked Pop-Pop.

"Jeffrey Charles Schafer, where are your manners?" my mother scolded.

Pop-Pop reached over and tousled Jeff's hair. "What do you think?"

"I think you forgot," Jeff said.

Pop-Pop laughed, then turned to Granny and said, "Rita, it's warm in here. Why don't you have some water?" I figured Jeff was right. Pop-Pop didn't have an anniversary gift for Granny.

Granny looked at Pop-Pop and said, "Oh, Charlie, you didn't!"

I thought she meant, "Oh, Charlie, you didn't get me a gift!" But that's not what she meant at all. "Oh, Charlie," she repeated as she lifted her water glass to the light.

"Need your glasses to see it, old girl?" Pop-Pop asked.

"I certainly do not," Granny said as she put a spoon in the glass and took something out. She held up a sapphire and diamond ring for us to see.

While Granny was putting on the ring and thanking Pop-Pop, my mother told us that Pop-Pop had given Granny her engagement ring the same way over fifty years before. "He dropped it in her water glass when she wasn't looking and then said, 'Rita, it's warm in here. Why don't you have a drink of water?' "

I had no more doubts that my grandparents loved one another — and always had. I thought how lucky I would be if I had such a happy marriage some day. I was also thinking how lucky I was to have parents who loved one another.

Just then Pop-Pop said, "We've been married fifty years. But there's another couple at this table who have been married fifteen. Sharon, Jack, I wish you two the happiness that Rita and I have had."

"Here, here," I said as I raised my ginger ale in the toast.

My parents had thirty-five years to go. But that weekend I had no doubt that they'd make it.

# Fire!

By the time I was twelve my parents' marriage was in big trouble. In the last few months before they split up, I did whatever I could <u>not</u> to notice how unhappy they were with each other.

Fire!

One of the ways I tried to shut out my parents' constant arguing was to spend as much time as I could away from home. After school and on weekends I'd mostly hang out with Sunny doing the things most seventh-graders do: fooling around, doing homework, going to the beach with our friends, and baby-sitting. Sunny and I liked baby-sitting and we had some clients who called on us a lot. I especially liked to sit for Clover and Daffodil Austin who lived next door to me.

Even though my parents were fighting I wasn't afraid they'd get divorced. My big fear that fall was that our house would burn down.

For as long as I could remember I'd been afraid of fire. When I was little my mother didn't have to remind me not to play with matches. I wouldn't go near them! I didn't like when people lit candles either. And whenever I heard fire truck sirens I'd worry that my house was on fire.

I knew that I was more afraid of fire than most people, so I didn't talk about it much. But one day I began to think that my fear of fire wasn't so unreasonable after all.

It was a Sunday evening and my parents had invited the Winslows for a barbecue supper in our backyard.

I was a little worried that my parents would

start bickering in front of the Winslows, but things went along smoothly at first. Mom, Mrs. Winslow, Sunny, and I were inside skewering chicken and vegetables. My dad, Mr. Winslow, and Jeff were in the backyard in charge of the grill.

Through the kitchen window I saw my dad light the coals. I always hated the big *swoosh* of fire when the fluid is lit. I kept an eye on the flames that were darting out of the grill.

"Are you finished skewering the peppers and onions?" my mother asked me.

"Almost," I mumbled distractedly. The fire in the grill had subsided. Now my father was moving the coals around with his big barbecue fork. That was also dangerous, I thought. Suddenly a hot coal popped out of the grill and landed on a pile of newspapers. In an instant the papers were in flames.

*"Fire!"* I screamed. My mother was already running out the door with the pitcher of iced tea. Sunny and her mother also grabbed liquids. But I was too panicky to act sensibly. Sunny later told me that I ran outside with them and just stood there screaming, "Fire! Fire!" while she and the adults easily put out the flames.

I do remember all of us standing around the charred papers. "Wow!" Jeff said. "That was neato."

"Neato?" I shouted at him. "The house could have burned down! The whole neighborhood could have been destroyed! People could have been killed! What's so 'neato' about that?"

"Calm down, Dawn," my dad said. "It was just a little fire. Everything's under control."

"It was an accident," my mother added.

"Right," my father mumbled to my mother. "Some accident. You said you were going to take those newspapers to the garage."

"And who knocked the hot coal out of the grill?" my mother asked.

They glared at one another for a second before remembering they had company and a meal to prepare. Things returned to normal for the rest of the evening. Normal for everyone but me. I was busy figuring out how I could protect our home and family from another accidental fire.

Before I went to bed that night I made a list of the steps I would take to insure our safety.

FIRE PREVENTION IN
THE SCHAFER HOME

- Check batteries in smoke alarms
- Put fire extinguisher in the kitchen and in the backyard (near barbecue grill).

- Plan and post evacuation routes
- Conduct fire drills.
- Practice opening and climbing out bedroom windows with eyes closed.
- Put important papers and family photos in a fireproof box.

I began fire prevention instruction at dinner the next evening. First, I read my checklist aloud so Jeff and our parents would have an overview of what we would be doing.

"How come I have to close my eyes when I climb out the window?" Jeff asked.

"Because during a fire there might be a lot of smoke and you wouldn't be able to see," I explained.

"Oh," Jeff said as he pushed back his chair. "I'll go try it."

"Eat your dinner first," my mother said.

"What if a fire starts right now and I don't know how to get out?" Jeff asked.

"Jeff, if a fire started right now," my father said, "it wouldn't make a lot of sense to go to our bedrooms and climb out the window with our eyes closed. We could go out the back door."

"It would sure make sense if the back door was on fire!" Jeff said with a grin. "Gotcha!"

"In that case, please use the front door rather than climbing out the window with your eyes closed," my father said.

"We'll work on escape routes later," I said. "Now, Jeff, here's a question. What would you take with you if there was a fire in the house?"

"Oh, that's easy," he replied. "First my video games and model airplanes. Oh yeah, and my bank. Definitely my bank. And — "

"Nope," I said. "Wrong answer. You know what you should take?"

"Don't say clothes, Dawn. My video games are more important."

"The correct answer is, don't take *anything*. When you are escaping a fire just get yourself out. Don't worry about your stuff."

"Dawn's right, Jeff," my mother added. I flashed her a thank-you smile.

"You mean you just let all your stuff burn?" Jeff said in amazement.

"It's the safe thing to do," I told him.

My mother assured me that the batteries in the smoke alarms were okay.

My father said I was right about putting important documents in a fireproof box and that ours were in one.

Before we left the table my parents promised

to buy two fire extinguishers.

While my father and I cleared the table Jeff went to his room to do homework and my mother made a phone call. After I put the dishes in the dishwasher, I sat at the kitchen table. I drew the layout of our house and added arrows to indicate the evacuation routes to take if there were a fire in the front of the house.

My mother came into the kitchen for a cup of tea. She looked over my shoulder and asked, "How's it going?"

"I'll make a chart with different evacuation routes in case of a fire in the back of the house," I told her.

"What if the fire is in the hall?" she asked.

"Good thinking, Mom," I said. "I'll make one for that, too."

"Don't encourage her," my father told my mother. I saw him give her an evil look as if it were her fault that I was trying to save their lives.

That night I stayed awake until I was sure that Jeff was asleep and my parents were in bed. Then I stood in the front hall and screamed at the top of my lungs, "Fire! Fire! Fire in the kitchen!" I made my old Minnie Mouse alarm clock go off at Jeff's door to be certain that he woke up. My parents rushed out of their room.

"What do you think you're doing?" my father asked. "It's almost midnight. You have school tomorrow."

"This is a fire drill," I explained. "You're supposed to go out the front door if there's a fire in the kitchen."

"Dawn, you can't expect me to go outside in my nightgown," my mother said.

"You're getting a little carried away here," my father added. "This really isn't necessary."

"Not necessary?" I cried in disbelief. "Jeff is sleeping through the fire drill. If that happened when there was a real fire — "

Just then the front doorbell rang.

"You probably woke the neighbors," my mother said.

"Dawn, you better answer it," my father said. "You're the only one who's properly dressed."

I ran to the door all the while thinking that I would expand my fire prevention program to the whole block. I'd photocopy my list . . .

I opened the door. Jeff walked in. "I went out the window like you said," he told me, "but I kept my eyes open."

Looking over his shoulder I saw that he was carrying his Gameboy behind his back. I didn't mention it. After all, he was the only one in the family who even responded to the fire drill.

"That was fun," Jeff told our parents. "Can we do it again tomorrow night? Is it my turn to decide when to shout fire?"

"No," my parents replied. That was the first thing I'd heard them agree about in weeks.

On Saturday I was in the kitchen reading the directions for using the new fire extinguisher when my dad returned from playing tennis. "I want to go over these directions with you," I said to him. "I already showed Jeff and Mom how to use it."

"I know how to use a fire extinguisher, Sunshine," he said.

"Well, okay, if you're really sure you know how."

"What's going on here today?" he asked.

"I'm baby-sitting for the Austins in a few minutes."

"You mean there won't be any fire prevention lessons today?" he asked with a grin.

"I guess not. But you should all review the evacuation routes. They're on the refrigerator door so you can look at them a lot."

Jeff wandered into the room. "I already know them by heart," he said.

Just before I left for my sitting job my mother came into the kitchen. She took something out of the fridge, stopped to look at the evacuation charts, just the way I'd planned, and said, "Well, let's see, what shall we have for dinner tonight? Barbecued kitchen or broiled living room?"

Jeff totally cracked up. "Now that's funny, Mom," he said. "That's *really* funny. Let me tell you why."

I had to laugh myself. Instead of fire prevention my parents were going to get a not-very-funny lecture on what makes a joke funny.

Since the Austins live in the house next to ours I only had to walk across our two yards to get to my sitting job. Five-year-old Clover burst out of the front door and ran to me shouting, "Dawn's here!" Eight-year-old Daffodil was right behind her.

"Can we play school, Dawn?" Clover asked as I led the girls inside. "We'll be the students and you be the teacher." Clover was five and had just started kindergarten, so she was pretty enthusiastic about school.

"I don't want to play school," complained Daffodil. "That's boring. I want to paint with our new pencils. Dawn, wait until you see them. They're pencils that turn into paint when you make them wet."

"If we played school," I told Daffodil as we entered the house, "you could teach us how to use the pencils. You could be the teacher and Clover and I would be your students."

"Well, I guess that's okay," Daffodil said, "if I can be the teacher."

"Oh, boy," said Clover. "We're going to play school."

Mrs. Austin came into the living room. "Good going, Dawn. You're a master at negotiation. I think you should run for public office."

"I'll settle for baby-sitting," I told her.

She looked at her watch. "I better go or I'll be late."

"Did you leave me the phone number where I can reach you?" I asked.

"Oh, my goodness," she said. "I've been so distracted today I almost forgot." She searched through her purse and handed me a business card. "Some of my pieces are in a group show at this gallery," she explained. "Today's the opening. Mr. Austin and I will be there for the next two hours. Then we'll come right home."

Mrs. Austin is a first-class weaver. She weaves creative, interesting pieces from different colors and types of yarns. You can hardly walk in the living room because of the looms Mrs. Austin has set out for her work. I looked around at the pieces that were still in the looms. Even half-finished they looked great. "Your work is so beautiful," I told her.

"I'm sure the show will be a big success."

"I hope so," she said. "Maybe you'll go see it."

"I want to. Mom and Dad want to go, too. Can I keep the card?"

"Of course."

I stuck the card in my jeans pocket.

Mr. Austin entered the living room and said hello to me. "All set?" he asked his wife.

"I guess," she said.

"Relax, darling. The pieces you put in the show are sensational. People will love them."

Mrs. Austin looked into Mr. Austin's eyes and smiled. "Thank you," she said softly. She kissed him on the cheek.

Seeing how much the Austins loved and respected one another reminded me of what was missing in my parents' relationship lately. But I didn't want to think about my parents and their fights, so I was glad when Mr. and Mrs. Austin left and I was alone with my baby-sitting charges. If I kept busy with the kids I wouldn't have time to think about the troubles at home.

Clover and Daffodil had fun playing school with the new art supplies. So did I. One of the things I love about baby-sitting is how creative it can be. First you get to think up fun, interesting things for the kids to do and then you get to do the activities with them. Our "teacher," Ms. Daffodil, told us to each make a picture that illustrated our first names. "It doesn't have to be realistic, class," she instructed. "For example, I don't have to draw a picture of a daffodil for my name. I can just make an abstract painting with a lot of yellow and green in it." I was impressed with how sophisticated Daffodil was when it came to art.

When we had finished our pictures and admired one another's work, Daffodil said, "Now, class, we will have physical education period." She leaned over and whispered to me, "Can we have it outside, Dawn?"

I nodded yes and our "teacher" led us out to the backyard. First we touched our toes ten times (with straight legs), then we played jump rope. After we'd all had a couple of turns jumping, Clover asked, "Teacher, when can we have snacks?"

Daffodil looked at me and I gave her the okay sign. "Snack time is right now, class," she said. "Line up behind me." We marched into the kitchen. "Dawn, you're in charge of snacks today."

"Okay, teacher," I said. I opened the refrigerator and looked around. "Today for snacks we are having apples and cheese."

"And chocolate chip cookies," added Daffodil.

"And chocolate chip cookies," I agreed.

We sat around the table to eat our snacks. "I like this school even better than kindergarten," Clover said.

Ms. Daffodil was smiling and looking very pleased with herself.

Suddenly I smelled something funny in the air. Was it smoke? I sniffed again. It *was* smoke. I looked around the kitchen. I didn't see any sign of fire. Without letting the kids know what I was doing I quickly walked around the kitchen and checked the stove, toaster oven, and coffee pot. They were turned off. Only a minute had passed since I first smelled the smoke, but now I could see that the room was getting smoky.

"What smells so funny?" asked Daffodil.

"My eyes sting," complained Clover.

I closed the door between the living room and the kitchen. "Let's go, girls," I said in a calm, authoritative voice. "We're leaving the house right now."

They heard the seriousness in my voice and reached for my hands. I led them through the nearest safe exit — the kitchen door.

We were walking quickly through their yard toward my backyard when Daffodil asked, "Is my house on fire?" Tears were gathering in her eyes.

"Something's making that smoke," I said. "But I don't know what."

Clover pulled on my hand and shrieked, "I want to go back and get my dolly!"

I remembered that my purse was in the house, too. In it were pictures of my friends, my school identification card, and ten dollars. Before I could worry too much about my own stuff, I remembered that *everything* belonging to the Austins was in that house, including Mrs. Austin's looms, her supplies, her finished pieces. Would everything connected with Mrs. Austin's art career be destroyed?

"We aren't going back inside for anything," I said firmly. "We're going to my house." I held tight to their hands and led them into my kitchen. My mother noticed us coming in and called from the living room, "Hi, girls. Glad you came by. I'll be right there." Before I even told my mother that the Austins' house was on fire, I picked up the phone.

"Are you going to call my mom and dad and tell them?" Daffodil asked.

"I want to talk to Mommy," Clover said.

Both girls began to cry. I couldn't blame them.

I dialed 911. "First I have to call the fire department," I told them.

My mother came into the kitchen while I was talking to the 911 operator. She smiled at Clover and Daffodil and said, "I see you girls are having a fire drill, too."

I pointed out the kitchen window and my mother saw the smoke pouring out of the Austins' kitchen door. She looked at me curiously, and I nodded as I gave the Austins' address to the operator.

When I finished that call I said to Clover and Daffodil, "Now we'll call your mother and father and tell them about the smoke and that the fire department is coming." I pulled the gallery business card out of my pocket and dialed the phone number printed at the bottom.

While I was waiting for Mrs. Austin to come to the phone, I told my mother how we had smelled smoke in the kitchen. She ran to the living room to tell my father what was going on.

I knew that the first thing to tell Mrs. Austin was that her children were okay. So when she came to the phone I said, "Mrs. Austin, it's Dawn. Clover and Daffodil are at my house."

Before I could tell her about the smoke she said, "Dawn, I was frightened! When the gallery owner said I had a phone call I thought there was an emergency. I'm so relieved. Listen, as long as your folks don't mind, it's fine if the girls play at your place."

I didn't want to upset Mrs. Austin, but I had to tell her that there *was* an emergency. "I brought them over here," I said, "because I smelled smoke in your kitchen. I called the fire department."

I heard Mrs. Austin gasp. Then the wail of fire sirens racing up our block could be heard. "The fire trucks are already here," I told her.

"Are you sure the girls are okay?" Mrs. Austin asked. She was so frightened that she sounded out of breath.

"Clover and Daffodil are standing right next to me," I said.

"Our house is on fire!" Daffodil yelled toward the phone.

"Mommy, I want my dolly," Clover cried.

"Don't let them go back in the house, Dawn," Mrs. Austin said.

"I won't," I promised.

"We'll be right there." Mrs. Austin hung up the phone.

By now my mother and father were in the kitchen with me and the girls. We ran out to the yard to watch their house.

The firefighters broke the kitchen windows and black, billowing smoke poured out through the holes. A crowd of neighbors had gathered on the sidewalk in front of the house and firefighters were directing them to the other side of the street. Any second I expected that beautiful home to burst into flames as the pile of newspapers did in our backyard.

The girls stood quietly on either side of me and held tightly to my hands. I talked to them in a calm, reassuring voice. First, I commented on how fast the firefighters had gotten there and how they knew just what to do to put out the fire. Then I reminded them that their mother and father were on their way home.

A few minutes later the Austins' car pulled into our driveway. Mr. Austin ran across the yard toward the firefighters while Mrs. Austin rushed to our house.

She squatted down and embraced her girls, then looked up at me. Tears were streaming down her cheeks. "Thank you,

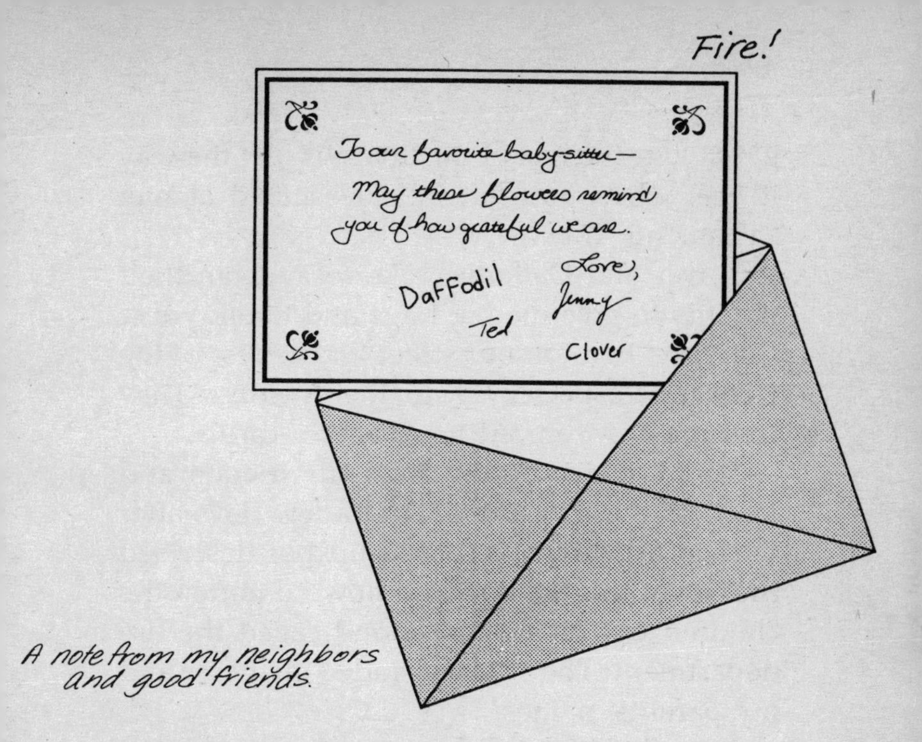

To our favorite baby-sitter—
May these flowers remind
you of how grateful we are.
Love,
Daffodil
Jenny
Ted
Clover


A note from my neighbors and good friends.

Dawn," she said. "Thank you so much."

A few minutes later Mr. Austin joined us. "The firefighters believe it was an electrical fire caused by faulty wiring," he said. "The fire was confined to the kitchen. Everything else is okay."

"What about the looms and all my work?" Mrs. Austin whispered.

"The door was closed between the kitchen and the living room," he replied, "so your supplies and looms are okay." I was glad I'd thought to close that door.

"Is my dolly burned? And my dollhouse?" Clover asked.

"The kitchen is a mess," Mr. Austin told the

girls, "but the rest of the house is just the way it was when you left it." He smiled at me. "Thanks to Dawn."

Clover and Daffodil broke away from their parents to give me big hugs and thank yous.

I was a hero on our street for the rest of the weekend, especially with the Austins. They sent me a dozen red roses with a card.

On Monday, Sunny told our friends and teachers what I'd done. And a few days after that an article in the weekly paper described the fire at the Austins' and how I'd gotten the children out of the house and called the fire department. The article included my name and my parents' names.

"Hey," Jeff complained when my dad showed him the article, "how come my name's not here? I'm her brother. Don't I count?"

"Sure you do," I said. "But they just mention parents' names for this kind of thing."

"If it were a longer article they would have talked about you, too," my dad assured him.

"I wish I'd been here for the fire," Jeff said for about the millionth time in three days, "and not at that dumb old soccer game. We didn't even win."

I was glad Jeff was the one who answered the phone the day the mayor's office called me. "What'd they want?" he asked after I hung up the phone. "Did you talk to the mayor?"

"I talked to the mayor's assistant," I told him. "He said that I'm one of this month's community heroes."

"They'll put your picture in the paper," Jeff said.

"Our whole family is invited to the ceremony at city hall next Saturday," I went on. "We'll meet the mayor."

Saturday morning we dressed in our best clothes for the ceremony. Jeff didn't even complain about having to wear a tie.

A young man was waiting for us in the lobby. "I'm Clyde Pearson," he said. "You must be Dawn. We spoke on the phone." While Mr. Pearson led us to the reception room I introduced him to the rest of my family.

I was surprised to see a crowd of people in the reception room. Mr. Pearson had said that the medals were being awarded at a private ceremony and that only one other community hero was being honored that month. He introduced us to Mrs. Marjorie Hughes and explained that she was being honored for being a foster parent. "Mrs. Hughes raised children who didn't have parents or relatives to take care of them," he explained. "She's been a mother to twenty children."

"Twenty kids!" Jeff exclaimed. "That's like the Old Woman Who Lived in a Shoe."

Mrs. Hughes laughed at that and told us that she hadn't taken care of them all at once. "The most I had at one time was six," she said.

"But as soon as one child was grown up and out of the house she'd take in another," Mr. Pearson explained. "In forty years it added up to twenty kids. And every one of them went to college."

"Fourteen of them are here today," Mrs. Hughes said proudly. "Some of them with spouses and their own children. They've already made me a grandmother seventeen times over. Five of those grandchildren are named after me."

I didn't feel like I was such a big hero when I thought of all the work and love that Mrs. Hughes had given to her foster children. I had led two kids out of a house and made a phone call. This had taken about five minutes. Mrs. Hughes had cared for kids day in and day out for forty years.

She was telling me how her children were taking her out for a special luncheon after the ceremony, when the mayor entered the room. The mayor was friendly and shook everybody's hand. I could see that Jeff was particularly impressed by that.

The mayor directed Mrs. Hughes and me to the front of the room to stand on either side of her at the podium. The people in the room became very quiet.

The mayor talked about the history of the community hero medal and mentioned some people who had received it in the past. Then she made a nice speech about Mrs. Hughes and put the medal around her neck. Everyone in the room, except Mrs. Hughes, clapped. I felt honored to be given a medal in the same ceremony as Mrs. Hughes.

Before the mayor hung the medal around my neck she described what I did during the fire at the Austins'. She ended her speech about me by saying, "Dawn Read Schafer, you acted wisely and bravely in a time of crisis. We are proud to have you as a citizen of Palo City."

I shook the mayor's hand and said thank you.

On the way home in the car my father joked that I'd probably drive them crazier than ever with fire drills.

My mother said, "I'm glad that Dawn has made us more aware of fire prevention and safety. We should have put a fire extinguisher in the kitchen years ago."

Jeff whispered in my ear, "Let's have a fire drill tonight. We'll surprise Mom and Dad."

"Not tonight," I whispered back. "We've had enough fire drills for awhile."

Oddly, I wasn't as afraid of fires as I had been before the fire at the Austins'. For one thing I saw how quickly the fire department responded to a call. For another I knew that in an emergency I could remain calm and act sensibly. But mainly I didn't think much about fires because my parents were fighting more than ever. Within a few weeks of the awards ceremony they told me they were separating.

A fire could have destroyed our home and possessions. But my parents' divorce destroyed our family. We would no longer be the family unit of Mom, Dad, Jeff, and Dawn. And there was nothing I could do about it. I couldn't make out a checklist of things to do for Divorce Prevention in the Schafer Home. I had drilled my family on what to do in case of fire. But there was no way to prepare for what to do in case of divorce.

Not long after I received the community hero medal I moved to Stoneybrook, Connecticut, a town on the other side of the country from the city that had honored me. I didn't know then how many challenges I would face as I tried to adjust to a new life, or how much I would miss my old one.

THE PALO CITY POST

Local Heroes

Community Hero medals awarded to Ms. Dawn Read Schafer and Mrs. Marjorie Hughes.

*The proudest day of my life.*

# A New Life on the East Coast

*When I was thirteen I did something that I am not proud of. Instead of doing the right thing when I was baby-sitting, I did the wrong thing. This is the first time I've told anyone what I did.*

That year I moved from the Pacific Ocean to the Atlantic Ocean. I adjusted pretty well to the big changes in my life, mostly because of the Baby-sitters Club and my new best friend, Mary Anne Spier.

The shameful incident I mentioned happened just a few months after I moved to Stoneybrook when I was still a new member of the Baby-sitters Club and before the wedding that made Mary Anne and me stepsisters.

On a warm spring afternoon, I'd just finished a baby-sitting job for the Barretts and was on my way to a Baby-sitters Club meeting. It was the first warm sunny day after three cold and rainy ones. I wanted to take my time and enjoy the balmy spring weather, but I had to rush if I were going to be at the meeting when it started at five-thirty. The BSC president, Kristy Thomas, does not tolerate lateness.

As I turned the corner onto Claudia's block I saw Mary Anne ahead of me. I ran to catch up to her. "Isn't this great?" I said, gesturing to the blue sky. "We finally have some decent weather."

"I love that it's warm again," Mary Anne replied.

"Mary Anne, you would love the weather in Palo City," I said. "We have one season — summer. It's great."

"I'd miss the other seasons. I like them all. Even winter. Snow is so pretty."

I'd just endured my first New England winter and hated it.

Fortunately the so-called "joys of winter" were the only things Mary Anne and I disagreed about. We were becoming best friends, especially now that my mother and her father were dating. Here's what's wonderful. Mary Anne and I figured out that my mother and her father were high school sweethearts. Their high school yearbooks, with romantic handwritten messages to one another, provided the clue. They'd gone their separate ways after high school and hadn't seen or spoken to one another in years. But when they re-met (thanks to me and Mary Anne) they fell in love all over again.

Mary Anne and I agreed that our parents were good for one another. I was glad my mother was happy living in Stoneybrook. I was pretty happy, too. I liked my new friends, especially Mary Anne. But I was homesick for California, and not just for the weather. I missed my friends and my old school. But mostly I missed Dad. Jeff felt the same way. A good chunk of our lives was missing, and there wasn't any way we could get it back. You can't see your dad on weekends when he lives three thousand miles away.

I didn't talk to Mary Anne about how much I missed my father. First of all, because she's so sensitive and kind that she might just burst into tears over it. Secondly, because Mary Anne's mother had died when Mary Anne was just a baby. I'd be seeing my father during the summer, but there was no way Mary Anne was ever going to see her mother again.

Anyway, I was thinking about Dad as we climbed the stairs to Claudia's room for the BSC meeting because I'd just been sitting for the Barrett kids — Buddy, Suzi, and Marnie. The Barretts were new clients. Mrs. Barrett had just divorced the children's father and was having trouble managing everything on her own. Sitting at the Barretts' usually meant picking up the house, bathing the kids, and feeding them. And those kids — especially Suzi and Buddy — were confused about the divorce. I knew how they felt from personal experience, so I could help them with that.

When Mary Anne and I walked into Claudia's room Kristy was already in her position of power, Claudia's director's chair. Kristy looked at us and then at the clock, which read 5:28, as if to say, "You were *almost* late."

"Hi, Kristy," I said. "How's it going?"

"Good," she answered in her let's-get-down-to-business voice. "Mary Anne, the record book is on the bed. Dawn, why don't you read the notebook."

I gave Claudia and Stacey a little wave.

"Stacey, are you ready to collect the dues?" Kristy asked. Stacey held up the manila envelope she used for our weekly dues.

At exactly five-thirty, Kristy said, "This Baby-sitters Club meeting will come to order. Stacey will collect the dues."

We forked over our money. "The total in the treasury is thirteen-fifty," Stacey reported.

"Does anyone need supplies for their Kid-Kits?" asked Kristy.

I was about to say I needed a new set of Magic Markers for mine when the phone rang. "Hello, Baby-sitters Club," Kristy said into the receiver.

For the next twenty minutes we answered the phone and booked jobs. In between phone calls we discussed who needed what for their Kid-Kits.

When that had been settled Kristy said, "Today I'm going over some basic rules of baby-sitting."

"We've done that a hundred times already," Stacey said.

"I don't think Dawn ever wrote them down." She looked at me. I shook my head no. "It's good for all of us to review these rules," Kristy concluded.

I wanted to remind Kristy that I'd been baby-sitting for a couple of years *before* I moved to Stoneybrook and became a member of the BSC. I even thought of reminding her that I'd been awarded the community hero medal because of my baby-sitting skills. But I kept my mouth shut and opened my notebook to write down Kristy's version of the rules for baby-sitting.

"Number one," she began, "be sure emergency phone numbers are listed near the phone."

"Including the phone number for the nearest take-out pizza joint," Stacey kidded.

Kristy ignored Stacey's comment, but the rest of us smiled at one another. Kristy continued. "Number two, have clear instructions on how to reach the parents while they are away from the house."

She looked in my direction to make sure I was writing the rules down. I was. "Number three," she said, "Ask parents about the children's meal and bedtimes. Also be sure you know any bedtime rituals."

"Rituals?" asked Claudia. "Like a séance or something?"

Kristy glared at her.

"I'm kidding, Kristy," Claudia said. "It's just that we know all this stuff."

"We are reviewing for Dawn," Kristy said

sharply. "Number four. Respect the privacy of your clients. Baby-sitters should not eavesdrop, snoop, or in any way violate the trust the client has placed in them."

"In other words, mind your own business," Stacey concluded.

"That's another way to put it," Kristy agreed.

The phone rang. I picked up the receiver and said, "Hello, Baby-sitters Club."

"Hello," a man's voice said. "My wife and I heard about your club from Dr. Johanssen. We need a sitter for our seven-year-old daughter, Sandra, this Saturday evening. We'd like to try your service."

I asked Mr. Lazar a few questions that we always ask new clients and told him I would call back in a few minutes to tell him if we could take the job.

When I hung up I told the others about the new client and that Dr. Johanssen had recommended us.

"Dr. Johanssen would never give our name out to someone she didn't approve of," Kristy said, "so I guess it's all right to take them on as clients. Who's free to sit Saturday night?"

Mary Anne checked the record book. "Dawn's the only one who doesn't have a job."

I thought quickly. Saturday night. I was

pretty sure Mom would go out with Mr. Spier, but I wouldn't have to stay with Jeff because he was going to sleep over at the Pikes'. "I'll do it," I said.

We agreed that I would sit for the new clients.

I called Mr. Lazar back and got the details for the job. Before I left the meeting Stacey gave me money from the treasury to buy new Magic Markers for my Kid-Kit.

I felt great as I walked home. The Baby-sitters Club had trusted me with a new client.

My job at the Lazars' began at six o'clock. Since it was my first job at their house I made sure to arrive a few minutes early.

Mrs. Lazar answered the door. She was dressed for an evening out. A bright-eyed little girl in jeans and a T-shirt was half-hiding behind her mother's skirt.

"Hi," I said. "I'm Dawn Schafer from the Baby-sitters Club." I smiled at the girl and asked, "Are you Sandra?"

The girl nodded and moved out from behind her mother.

"I'm glad you came a little early, Dawn," Mrs. Lazar said. "Since it's the first time you've been here there's a lot to tell you. Come on in and we'll get started."

I followed Mrs. Lazar through the living room, down a hall, and into the kitchen. Sandra, who was walking beside me, pointed to my Kid-Kit and asked, "What's in there?"

"This is my Kid-Kit," I explained. "It's filled with games and other things for us to do."

"What a wonderful idea," Mrs. Lazar said.

"Can we play with it now?" Sandra asked.

"First I have to talk to Dawn," Mrs. Lazar said. "After dinner and a half hour of homework, you can play with the toys that Dawn brought."

Sandra frowned and complained, "That's a long time to wait."

"Maybe Sandra could see what's in the Kid-Kit now while we talk," I said.

"That's a good idea," Mrs. Lazar agreed.

I put the Kid-Kit on the table and Sandra looked through it while her mother told me what to prepare for supper, where the emergency numbers were listed, and how to reach her and her husband in an emergency. "Sandra will show you what she has for homework," Mrs. Lazar explained. "Give her as much help as she needs with it. Bedtime is at nine o'clock on weekend nights and we always have a bedtime story."

"There're books in the Kid-Kit," Sandra said. "Can Dawn read me one of those?"

Mrs. Lazar said yes to her daughter and smiled at me. "I have a feeling you and Sandra will do just fine together," she said. "Now let's go into the living room so I can show you where to write down messages."

Sandra closed up the Kid-Kit and we followed her mother into the living room. Mrs. Lazar showed me a pad on the desk where I should write down phone messages. "In the past sitters haven't been very good at writing down messages," she said. "It's led to some mix-ups that I would rather have avoided."

I assured her that I would take careful messages.

A few minutes later the Lazars left for the evening and I was alone with Sandra.

First we made dinner together. Sandra tore up the lettuce for the salad while I cooked noodles. Then Sandra decided to pretend we were on a television cooking show. While I made the cheese sauce and added it to our noodles she explained what I was doing for the make-believe television cameras. She called her cooking show *The Easy TV Cooking Show*. It was great fun and I was impressed that Sandra was so clever.

During dinner Sandra asked, "Can we play with the Kid-Kit after supper?"

I smiled at her and asked, "What do you think?"

"I think I have to do a half hour of homework first," she said with a frown.

"We'll make your homework fun to do," I told her. "You'll see."

We sat on the living room rug in front of the coffee table. Sandra opened up her reading workbook and put it on the table. "I have to read a story and answer questions," she said glumly.

"Why don't you read the story out loud," I said.

"Will you help me with words I don't know?"

"Of course I will."

Sandra flashed me a dimpled smile. "Thanks," she said. Even though she smiled I could sense that she was getting nervous about reading out loud. When she started to read the story I understood why. Most kids her age could easily read a simple story such as the one we were working on. But Sandra couldn't. For example, she read "sing" for "swing" and "saw" for "was."

The phone rang. "You read over what we've read so far while I get the phone," I told Sandra.

I went to the desk and picked up the receiver. "Lazar residence," I said.

"Hello," a woman's voice at the other end said, "is Janice there?"

I sat down at the desk and placed the message pad and pencil in front of me.

"Mrs. Lazar isn't in this evening," I said. "Would you like to leave a message?"

"Yes. Tell her that Mrs. Saunders called about — " There was a pause on the phone line. "I have another call," she said. "Please hold on."

While I waited I wrote down Mrs. Saunders' name and the time she called. As I sat there waiting for her to come back on the line I idly flipped through the papers in front of me. There were bills, checking statements, and letters. I noticed that one of the letters was from Stoneybrook Elementary. I saw that it was about Sandra. I read it.

Dear Mr. and Mrs. Lazar,

I have met with the learning specialist, Dr. Jackson, who, with your permission, recently tested Sandra. I've also reviewed Sandra's work in Ms. Cahill's classroom. We strongly recommend that Sandra repeat second grade. We are confident that with extra help at both school and home Sandra will make significant progress in her reading and math skills during the next school year.

Please call me at your earliest convenience

to set up a meeting with the reading specialist and Ms. Cahill.

Sincerely,
Dana Livingston
Principal

Repeat second grade? Poor Sandra, I thought. It must be awful to have to repeat a grade. I knew I'd have hated to have to stay behind while my friends went on to the next grade.

Mrs. Saunders' voice on the phone interrupted my thoughts. "Sorry that took so long," she said.

"That's okay."

"Tell Janice that the Audubon Society executive meeting for tomorrow night has been canceled. Jack has been called out of town on a family emergency. I'll call Janice as soon as the meeting's been rescheduled. Do you have all that?"

I repeated what she'd told me to be sure I had it right. After I hung up the phone I finished writing the message down. *Mrs. Saunders called to say Audubon meeting tomorrow night canceled. Jack had family emergency. Mrs. S. will call back when rescheduled.*

"Dawn, there're a bunch of words here I can't read," Sandra said.

"Okay," I said. "I'll be right there."

I left the message by the phone. I also made sure that the letter I'd read from Stoneybrook Elementary School was where it was when I'd first sat down. I didn't want the Lazars to know I'd been reading their mail.

I sat next to Sandra on the rug. "Let's start the story from the beginning," I said. "I'll read and you follow with your finger. Then it will be your turn. Okay?"

I was very patient with Sandra and we finished her homework.

"I don't read good," Sandra said.

"You will someday," I assured her. "It just takes lots of time and practice."

Poor Sandra, I thought. She must see that her friends have already learned how to read. That must make her feel frustrated. I was determined to make her feel special.

When I was tucking her into bed I told her, "I had fun baby-sitting for you. Your idea of pretending we were on TV when we were cooking was just great. I'm going to do that with other kids I sit for. And I'll tell them it was your idea."

"You're the best baby-sitter I ever had," Sandra said.

"Thanks."

When I went downstairs again I checked to see that the kitchen was cleaned up. Then I did a quick once-over of the living room. I packed up the Kid-Kit and straightened out the couch cushions. I double-checked that the phone message I'd written down was easy to read and free of spelling errors. I thought of reading the letter about Sandra, but didn't.

I knew I'd broken the "never snoop" rule of baby-sitting and my conscience had started to bother me. Well, I rationalized to myself, if I'm sitting for Sandra I should know that she has to repeat second grade. It's a special problem, like divorced parents. Look how knowing that the Barrett kids' parents are divorced helps me to help them. I'll be an even better sitter for Sandra because I know she's going to repeat second grade. Then I remembered that Mrs. Barrett had told me about the divorce and that I had learned about Sandra by snooping. My noisy conscience started nagging at me again.

A few minutes later the Lazars returned. When Mrs. Lazar asked me how the evening had gone I told her everything that we'd done and that a message from Mrs. Saunders was on the desk.

"I'm very impressed with you and your club," she said. "We'll call on you again soon."

She paid me and I left.

Seeing Mrs. Lazar face-to-face made me feel

creepy and more guilty than ever. I'd read the private letter about Sandra. As I put on my coat I told my conscience, "No one knows I did it and I won't tell anyone. I got away with it. So what's the big deal?"

A week later school let out for the year. Before our first BSC meeting of summer vacation we had a party in Claudia's room. We were all gabbing, laughing, and feeling great. Even Kristy was in a loose and slightly wild mood. But the second the clock turned to five-thirty she became no-nonsense Kristy again. The rest of us did the best we could to calm down, too.

*Ring.*

I picked up the phone. "Hello, Baby-sitters Club."

It was Mrs. Lazar asking for a sitter for the following afternoon. "I hope you're free to sit, Dawn," she said. "Sandra's especially requesting you."

"I liked sitting for her," I told Mrs. Lazar. "But I know that Sandra will like the other sitters in the club, too. We'll check the schedule and call you right back to tell you which

*A summer party with my new BSC friends.*

sitter will be taking the job." I secretly hoped it would be me.

As it turned out Claudia and I were both free to sit the next afternoon. But since the Lazars were new clients and they'd asked for me, we decided that I should take the job.

The next day after lunch I walked to the Lazars'.

Sandra opened the door. "Hi, Dawn," she said. "Did you tell the other kids about the television cooking show?"

"Sure I did," I answered. "It was a huge success with these three kids I sit for. Their names are Buddy, Suzi, and Marnie Barnett. We made microwave pizza. Buddy really hammed it up for the make-believe cameras."

"Did you tell them it was my idea?" Sandra asked.

"Absolutely."

We went into the kitchen where Mrs. Lazar was clearing up after lunch. "I'll be at the Audubon Society office," she said. "I left the number next to the phone on my desk."

"Can we cook something?" Sandra asked. "We like to pretend we're on television."

"You already had lunch," Mrs. Lazar answered as she finished her cleanup. "I was hoping you'd play out of doors. It's such a beautiful day."

"Maybe we could pretend cook," I told Sandra, "since we're on pretend television. We could do it in the yard. And we could make a sign with the name of the show. You could do drawings on it. I have a new set of Magic Markers in my Kid-Kit."

"Dawn, you have the best ideas," Sandra said.

"She certainly does," Mrs. Lazar said. She gave her daughter a hug. "But first, Miss Television Cook, a half hour of reading. Okay?"

"Oh, all right," Sandra said. "But can it be a book from the Kid-Kit?"

"That'd be fine. You and Dawn can take turns reading." She looked at me to be sure I understood that Sandra should do some of the reading herself. I smiled and nodded.

After Mrs. Lazar left, Sandra and I headed for the backyard with my Kid-Kit and the kitchen timer. The timer was Sandra's idea. She wanted to be sure that she didn't spend one second more than thirty minutes reading. We settled ourselves at the picnic table and I took out an easy-to-read book from the Kid-Kit. Sandra set the timer for thirty minutes.

When she saw the book I'd put in front of us on the table she said, "That's a Madeline book. I know that story. I read it already."

"Me, too," I said. "Madeline books were my favorites. And I still like to read them." I smiled at Sandra. "Sometimes it's easier to read a book when you know the story already."

"Okay," she said. "You start."

"I'll point to the words as I read," I said, "and you follow along."

After a few pages I said, "Now it's your turn."

Poor Sandra. She struggled with every word. I coaxed her and made encouraging comments, but she was miserable and kept asking how many minutes were left. I would have turned the reading session into a math session about how to read a timer, but I'd promised Sandra's mother that we'd read. So we stuck with the book.

"Even a dummy could read this book," Sandra said sadly. "I can't even read a word with three letters." She slammed the book shut. "I'm the dumbest kid in my class. I'll never learn to read."

I put my arm around her shoulder. "Don't get discouraged, Sandra. It has nothing to do with smart or dumb. It's a special problem. You'll work on your reading all summer. And doing second grade over is going to be a big help, too."

The instant the words were out of my mouth I knew I'd made a mistake. The look on Sandra's face told me that she didn't know she would be repeating second grade. "I'm going to be in the *third* grade," she said hesitantly. "I was already in second grade."

"Right," I said. "I remember now."

The timer went off.

"So we're finished with reading," I said cheerfully. "It's time for television cooking. What should we do first? Cook? Make the sign? Or make up a theme song for the show?"

"What's a theme song?" Sandra asked in a quiet voice.

"It's the song they play at the beginning and end of a television show," I said. "For example, *Sesame Street* has a theme song." I started singing the *Sesame Street* theme song and pretending I was singing it for a big audience. Soon Sandra joined in.

Then we made up lyrics for *The Easy TV Cooking Show.* We sang it with gestures to illustrate the words. Sandra was having fun. I hoped with all my heart that she had forgotten what I said about her repeating second grade.

Sandra was drawing pictures on *The Easy TV Cooking Show* sign when I saw that Mrs. Lazar was home. "Your mom's here," I said. "Let's sing the theme song for her."

Sandra jumped up from the table and ran across the yard to her mother calling, "Mommy, Mommy, Dawn said I have to go to second grade again."

Lights, camera, action!

My heart sank. I'd been found out. And I'd upset Sandra.

Mrs. Lazar squatted down to her daughter's height and said quietly, "Go up to your room, honey, and I'll be right there to talk to you. Okay?"

Sandra ran inside without looking back at me. I met Mrs. Lazar halfway across the yard. I didn't know what to say so I didn't say anything.

"I assume you found the letter from the school," she said gravely.

I nodded.

"We weren't planning on telling Sandra that she's repeating second grade until a few days before school starts in the fall." She spoke quietly, but I could hear the anger in her voice. "Sandra is a real worrier and there's a lot for her to worry about in this situation. She'll be separated from her friends and she'll be working with a special tutor. She's not going to understand that repeating second grade is good for her until she's experienced it. Now she has all summer to think about it and worry."

"I'm sorry," I said.

"I'm sure you are," Mrs. Lazar said. "But that won't make it any easier for Sandra, will it?"

"No."

I was feeling so ashamed and upset that I don't even remember being paid or leaving or anything else except that I probably said "I'm sorry" about a dozen times.

I didn't tell a soul what I'd done to Sandra. The only good thing about it was that I'd learned a lesson about snooping and people's right to their privacy. It was a lesson I'd never forget and I knew that I'd never do anything like that again. I only wish that I hadn't made life even harder for a little girl who was already having a difficult time.

Besides being ashamed I was afraid that Mrs. Lazar would call the BSC and complain about me and I'd be kicked out of the club.

Every time the phone rang during the next few meetings I felt my heartbeat jump. But Mrs. Lazar never called the BSC again, either to complain or to hire a sitter. We had a lot of new clients that summer and no one seemed to notice that we'd lost one. No one but me.

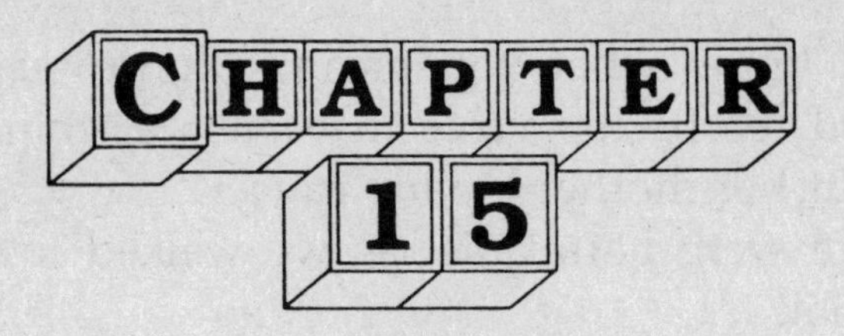


I finished my autobiography at ten o'clock on Thursday night. It was due on Friday. The last thing I did was make the cover. I drew an outline of the map of the United States (without Hawaii and Alaska) in black Magic Marker on light blue paper. In the middle of the country, from the Rocky Mountains to the Mississippi River, I printed my title: *The Life and Times of Dawn Read Schafer: Bicoastal Girl.* Next I pasted a snapshot on the west side of the country. It was of me at the beach with Jeff and Dad. Then on the east side of the country I placed a snapshot of me standing on a snowbank next to Jeff and my mom.

When I met Sunny to go to school the next morning I showed her the cover. "It's great," she said. "And your autobiography is so thick."

"Once I got started I just kept going," I told her. "I feel sort of older after thinking about all the things that have happened to me so far."

"I know what you mean," Sunny said. I could tell by her voice that she was thinking about her mother having cancer.

We were both quiet as we walked toward school.

Sunny broke the silence. "Do you want to read my autobiography?" she asked.

"If you'll read mine."

"Okay," she said with a big grin. "Let's share them after we get them back."

A wave of fear passed through me. Maybe Sunny wouldn't like me so much when she learned that I had read a baby-sitting client's private mail and ruined their daughter's summer. And how would Sunny feel, I wondered, when she read that I had been embarrassed by the way she dressed when her parents were hippies? And would she think I was stupid not to have seen that my parents were headed for a divorce? Would she think I was vain to be so proud of getting Clover and Daffodil Austin out of their house when I smelled the electrical fire?

We'd reached school. Before we went inside Sunny said, "Dawn, when you read my autobiography you're going to learn things about me that I've never told you."

"So are you," I said. "I wrote about something I did that I'm not proud of."

"Me, too. I hope you'll still like me after you read it."

"Me, too."

We were both laughing as we hurried across the schoolyard to our homeroom.

I was glad that Sunny was going to read my autobiography. I realized that what she read wouldn't change her feelings toward me. And that nothing she wrote in her autobiography would make me change mine. In fact, I was pretty sure that we'd be better friends than ever after we read one another's autobiographies.

I was unbearably nervous all weekend wondering how I would do on my first big assignment since I returned to school in California. What if our English teacher, Ms. Granger, didn't like it? I wondered if I should have written a short section about each year of my life instead of saying so much about a few incidents that were scattered over thirteen years.

It was a nerve-wracking weekend for Sunny, too. We decided that the only way to deal with our case of nerves was to go to the beach with Jill and Maggie on Sunday. Surfing helped me forget for awhile. And going to Maggie's house to preview a film that hadn't been released yet made some more time go by. The next thing I knew it was Monday morning and I was in first-period English class.

"Well, I had a busy weekend," Ms. Granger said. She gestured to the huge pile of notebooks and folders on her desk. "I must say I know a lot more about you guys than I did on Friday." She winked at us and smiled. "Over all, class, you did a fine job. I'm impressed with you as writers and as thoughtful human beings. Give yourselves a hand."

We all clapped.

"Now," she said, "I suppose you'd like to get your autobiographies back and see your grades."

We moaned.

"Ah, come on. It's not that bad. If you put the effort in your work, it'll show in your grade."

I still felt nervous. What if the effort I had put into my work didn't show?

I folded my hands so I wouldn't bite my nails while I waited through all the names that came before she called "Dawn Read Schafer."

I went to the front of the room and took my autobiography from Ms. Granger. She smiled as she handed me my book. Was that a good sign or was she smiling at me out of pity?

I rushed to my seat, put the book on my lap, and opened it. A note was paper-clipped to the inside cover.

From the desk of Janet Granger

Good work, Dawn. You told your life story by describing a few incidents in detail. Each incident had a strong plotline. I'm especially impressed with how you created suspense in the section "When I was thirteen." You're a good storyteller. It's great to have you back at Vista.

J. G.

Content: A-

Presentation: B

I sighed with relief. It must have been a pretty loud sigh because Ms. Granger and the whole class burst into laughter. I laughed, too. It was great being home.

L. GODWIN

**Ann M. Martin**

# About the Author

ANN MATTHEWS MARTIN was born on August 12, 1955. She grew up in Princeton, NJ, with her parents and her younger sister, Jane.

Although Ann used to be a teacher and then an editor of children's books, she's now a full-time writer. She gets the ideas for her books from many different places. Some are based on personal experiences. Others are based on childhood memories and feelings. Many are written about contemporary problems or events.

All of Ann's characters, even the members of the Baby-sitters Club, are made up. (So is Stoneybrook.) But many of her characters are based on real people. Sometimes Ann names her characters after people she knows, other times she chooses names she likes.

In addition to the Baby-sitters Club books, Ann Martin has written many other books for children. Her favorite is *Ten Kids, No Pets* because she loves big families and she loves animals. Her favorite Baby-sitters Club book is *Kristy's Big Day*. (By the way, Kristy is her favorite baby-sitter!)

Ann M. Martin now lives in New York. She has two cats, Mouse and Rosie (who's a boy, but that's a long story). Her hobbies are reading, sewing, and needlework — especially making clothes for children.

**Read all the books**
**about Dawn**
**in the Baby-sitters Club series**
**by Ann M. Martin**

\# 5 *Dawn and the Impossible Three*
Dawn thought she'd be baby-sitting — not *monster* sitting!

\# 9 *The Ghost at Dawn's House*
Does Dawn live in a haunted house?!?

#15 *Little Miss Stoneybrook . . . and Dawn*
Everyone in Stoneybrook has gone beauty-pageant crazy!

#23 *Dawn on the Coast*
Could Dawn be a California girl for good?

#31 *Dawn's Wicked Stepsister*
Dawn thought having a stepsister was going to be fun.

#37 *Dawn and the Older Boy*
Will Dawn's heart be broken by an older boy?

#44 *Dawn and the Big Sleepover*
One hundred kids, thirty pizzas — it's Dawn's biggest baby-sitting job ever!

#50 *Dawn's Big Date*
Will Dawn's date with Logan's cousin be a total disaster?

#57 *Dawn Saves the Planet*
Dawn's trying to do a good thing — but she's driving everyone crazy!

#64 *Dawn's Family Feud*
Family squabbles are one thing. But the Schafers and the Spiers are practically waging war!

#72 *Dawn and the We ♥ Kids Club*
Is Dawn's California baby-sitting club more popular than Stoneybrook's BSC?

#77 *Dawn and Whitney, Friends Forever*
Can Dawn be a baby-sitter and a friend?

#84 *Dawn and the School Spirit War*
How will Dawn stop SMS from becoming a school-spirit battlefield?

#88 *Farewell, Dawn*
This time, Dawn's going back to California for good.

Mysteries:

# 2 *Beware, Dawn*
Someone is playing pranks on Dawn when she's baby-sitting — and they're *not* funny.

# 7 *Dawn and the Disappearing Dogs*
Someone's been stealing dogs all over Stoneybrook!

#12 *Dawn and the Surfer Ghost*
When a local surfer mysteriously disappears, Dawn fears his ghost is haunting the beach.

#17 *Dawn and the Halloween Mystery*
This is one Fright Night Dawn will never forget!

Portrait Collection:

*Dawn's Book*
The California girl tells it all.

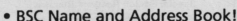